The Heir

V. Sackville-West

MINT EDITIONS

The Heir was first published in 1922.

This edition published by Mint Editions 2021.

ISBN 9781513135502 | E-ISBN 9781513212074

Published by Mint Editions®

MINT
EDITIONS

minteditionbooks.com

Publishing Director: Jennifer Newens
Design & Production: Rachel Lopez Metzger
Project Manager: Micaela Clark
Typesetting: Westchester Publishing Services

Contents

THE HEIR

I

M iss Chase lay on her immense red silk four-poster that reached as high as the ceiling. Her face was covered over by a sheet, but as she had a high, aristocratic nose, it raised the sheet into a ridge, ending in a point. Her hands could also be distinguished beneath the sheet, folded across her chest like the hands of an effigy; and her feet, tight together like the feet of an effigy, raised the sheet into two further points at the bottom of the bed. She was eighty-four years old, and she had been dead for twenty-four hours.

The room was darkened into a shadowy twilight. Outside, in a pale, golden sunshine, the birds twittered among the very young green of the trees. A thread of this sunshine, alive with golden dust-motes, sundered the curtain and struck out, horizontally, across the boards of the floor. One of the two men who were moving with all possible discretion about the room, paused to draw the curtains more completely together.

"Very annoying, this delay about the coffin," said Mr. Nutley. "However, I got off the telegrams to the papers in time, I hope, to get the funeral arrangements altered. It would be very awkward if people from London turned up for the funeral on Thursday instead of Friday— very awkward indeed. Of course, the local people wouldn't turn up; they would know the affair had had to be put off; but London people— they're so *scattered*. And they would be annoyed to find they had given up a whole day to a country funeral that wasn't to take place after all."

"I should think so, indeed," said Mr. Chase, peevishly. "I know the value of time well enough to appreciate that."

"Ah yes," Mr. Nutley replied with sympathy, "you're anxious to be back at Wolverhampton, I know. It's very annoying to have one's work cut into. And if *you* feel like that about it, when the old lady was your aunt, what would comparative strangers from London feel, if they had to waste a day?"

They both looked resentfully at the still figure under the sheet on the bed, but Mr. Chase could not help feeling that the solicitor was a little over-inclined to dot his i's in the avoidance of any possible hypocrisy. He reflected, however, that it was, in the long run, preferable to the opposite method of Mr. Farebrother, Nutley's senior partner, who was at times so evasive as to be positively unintelligible.

"Very tidy, everything. H'm—handkerchiefs, gloves, little bags of lavender in every drawer. Yes, just what I should have expected: she was a rare one for having everything spick and span. She'd go for the servants, tapping her stick sharp on the boards, if anything wasn't to her liking; and they all scuttled about as though they'd been wound up after she'd done with them. I don't know what you'll do with the old lady's clothes, Mr. Chase. They wouldn't fetch much, you know, with the exception of the lace. There's fine, real lace here, that ought to be worth something. It's all down in the heirloom book, and it'll have to be unpicked off the clothes. But for the rest, say twenty pounds. These silk dresses are made of good stuff, I should say," observed Mr. Nutley, fingering a row of black dresses that hung inside a cupboard, and that as he stirred them moved with the faint rustle of dried leaves; "take my advice, and give some to the housekeeper; that'll be of more value to you in the end than the few pounds you might get for them. Always get the servants on your side, is my axiom. However, it's your affair; you're the sole heir, and there's nobody to interfere." He said this with a sarcastic inflection detected only by himself; a warning note under the ostensible deference of his words as though daring Chase to assert his rights as the heir. "And, anyway," he concluded, "we're not likely to find anymore papers in here, so we're wasting time now. Shall we go down?"

"Wait a minute, listen: what's that noise out in the garden?"

"Oh, that! one of the peacocks screeching. There are at least fifty of the damned birds. Your aunt wouldn't have one of them killed, not one. They ruin a garden. Your aunt liked the garden, and she liked the peacocks, but she liked the peacocks better than the garden. Screech, screech—you'll soon do away with them. At least, I should say you *would* do away with them if you were going to live here. I can see you're a man of sense."

Mr. Chase drew Mr. Nutley and his volubility out on to the landing, closing the door behind him. The solicitor ruffled the sheaf of papers he carried in his hand, trying to peep between the sheets that were fastened together by an elastic band.

"Well," he said briskly, "if you're agreeable I think we might go downstairs and find Farebrother and Colonel Stanforth. You see, we are trying to save you all the time we possibly can. What about the old lady? do you want anyone sent in to sit with her?"

"I really don't know," said Chase, "what's usually done? you know more about these things than I do."

"Oh, as to that, I should think I ought to!" Nutley replied with a little self-satisfied smirk. "Perhaps you won't believe me, but most weeks I'm in a house with a corpse. There are usually relatives, of course, but in this case if you wanted anyone sent in to sit with the old lady, we should have to send a servant. Shall I call Fortune?"

"Perhaps you had better—but I don't know: Fortune is the butler, isn't he? Well, the butler told me all the servants were very busy."

"Then it might be as well not to disturb them? At any rate, the old lady won't run away," said Mr. Nutley jocosely.

"No, perhaps we needn't disturb them." Chase was relieved to escape the necessity of giving an order to a servant.

They went downstairs together.

"Hold on to the banisters, Mr. Chase; these polished stairs are very tricky. Fine old oak; solid steps too; but I prefer a drugget myself. Good gracious, how that peacock startled me! Look at it, sitting on the ledge outside the window. It's pecking at the panes with its beak. Shoo! you great gaudy thing." The solicitor flapped his arms at it, like a skinny crow beating its wings.

They stopped to look at the peacock, which, walking the outside ledge with spread tail, seemed to form part, both in colour and pattern, of the great heraldic window on the landing of the staircase. The sunlight streamed through the colours, and the square of sunlight on the boards was chequered with patches of violet, red, and indigo.

"Gaudy?" said Chase. "It's barbaric. Like jewels. Astonishing."

Mr. Nutley glanced at him with a faint contempt. Chase was a sandy, weakly-looking little man, with thin reddish hair, freckles, and washy blue eyes. He wore an old Norfolk jacket and trousers that did not match; Mr. Nutley, in his quick impatient mind, set him aside as reassuringly insignificant.

"Farebrother and Colonel Stanforth are in the library, I believe," Nutley suggested.

"Don't forget to introduce me to Colonel Stanforth," said Chase, dismayed at having to meet yet another stranger. "He was an intimate friend of my aunt's, wasn't he? Is he the only trustee?"

"The other one died and was never replaced. As for Colonel Stanforth being an intimate friend of the old lady, he was indeed; about the only friend she ever had; she frightened everybody else away," said Nutley, opening the library door.

"Ah, Mr. Chase!" Mr. Farebrother exclaimed in a relieved and propitiatory tone.

"We've been through all the drawers," Mr. Nutley said, his briskness redoubled in his partner's presence. "We've got all the necessary papers—they weren't even locked up—so now we can get to business. With any luck Mr. Chase ought to see himself back at Wolverhampton within the week, in spite of the delay over the funeral. I've told Mr. Chase that it isn't strictly correct to open the papers before the funeral is over, but that, having regard to his affairs in Wolverhampton, and in view of the fact that there are no other relatives whose susceptibilities we might offend, we are setting to work at once." He was bending over the table, sorting out the papers as he talked, but now he looked up and saw Chase still standing in embarrassment near the door. "Dear me, I was forgetting. Mr. Chase, you don't know Colonel Stanforth, your trustee, I think? Colonel Stanforth has lived outside the park gates all his life, and I wager he knows every acre of your estate better than you ever will yourself, Mr. Chase."

Mr. Farebrother, a round little rosy man in large spectacles, smiled benignly as Chase and Stanforth shook hands. He liked bringing the heir and the trustee together, but his pleasure was clouded by Nutley's last remark, suggesting as it did that Chase would never have the opportunity of learning his estate; he felt this remark to be in poor taste.

"Oh, come! I hope we shall have Mr. Chase with us for sometime," he said pleasantly, "although," he added, recollecting himself, "under such melancholy circumstances." He had never been known to make anymore direct allusion to death than that contained in this or similarly consecrated phrases. Mr. Nutley pounced instantly upon the evasion.

"After all, Farebrother, Chase never knew the old lady, remember. The melancholy part of it, to my mind, is the muddle the estate is in. Mortgaged up to the last shilling, and over-run with peacocks. Won't you come and sit at the table, Mr. Chase? Here's a pencil in case you want to make any notes."

Colonel Stanforth came up to the table at the same time. Chase shied away, and went to sit on the window-seat. Mr. Farebrother began a little preamble.

"We sent for you immediately, Mr. Chase; that is to say, Colonel Stanforth, who was on the spot at the moment of the regrettable event, communicated with us and with you simultaneously. We should like to welcome you, with all the sobriety required by the cloud which must hang over this occasion, to the estate which has been in the possession of your family for the past five hundred years. We should like to express our infinite regret at the embarrassments under which the estate will be found to labour. We should like to assure you—I am speaking now for my partner and myself—that our firm has been in no way responsible for the management of the estate. Miss Chase, your aunt, whom I immensely revered, was a lady of determined character and charitable impulses. . ."

"You mean, she was an obstinate old sentimentalist," said Mr. Nutley, losing his patience.

Mr. Farebrother looked gently pained.

"Charitable impulses," he repeated, "which she was always loth to modify. Colonel Stanforth will tell you that he has had many a discussion. . ." ("I should just think so," said Colonel Stanforth, "you could argue the hind leg off a donkey, but you couldn't budge Phillida Chase,") "there were questions of undesirable tenants and what not—I confess it saddens me to think of Blackboys so much encumbered. . ."

"Encumbered! My good man, the place will be in the market as soon as I can get it there," said Mr. Nutley, interrupting again, and tapping his pencil on the table.

"It would have been so pleasant," said Mr. Farebrother sighing, "if matters had been in an entirely satisfactory condition, and our duty towards Mr. Chase would have been so joyfully fulfilled. Your family, Mr. Chase, were Lords of the Manor of Blackboys long before any house was built upon this site. The snapping of such a chain of tradition. . ."

"Out of date, out of date, my good man," said Nutley, full of contempt and surprisingly spiteful.

"Let's get on to the will," suggested Stanforth.

Mr. Nutley produced it with alacrity.

"Dear, dear," said Mr. Farebrother, wiping his spectacles. The reading of a will was to him always a painful proceeding. It was indeed an unkind fate which had cast one of his amiable and conciliatory nature into the melancholy regions of the law.

"It's very short," said Nutley, and read it aloud.

After providing for a legacy of five hundred pounds to the butler, John Fortune, in recognition of his long and devoted service, and for a legacy of two hundred and fifty pounds to her friend Edward Stanforth "in anticipation of services to be rendered after my death," the testator devised the Manor of Blackboys and the whole of the Blackboys Estate and all other messuages tenements hereditaments and premises situate in the counties of Kent and Sussex and elsewhere and all other estates and effects whatsoever and wheresoever both real and personal to her nephew Peregrine Chase at present of Wolverhampton.

"Sensible woman—she got a solicitor to draw up her will," said Mr. Nutley as he ended; "no side-tracks, no ambiguities, no bother. Sensible woman. Now we can get to work."

"Ah, dear!" said Mr. Farebrother in wistful reminiscence, "how well I remember the day Miss Chase sent for me to assist her in the making of that will; it was just such a day as this, and after I had been waiting a little while she came into the room, a black lace cap on her white hair, and her beautiful hands leaning on the top of her stick—she had very beautiful hands, your aunt, Mr. Chase, beautiful cool ivory hands—and I remember she was singularly gracious, singularly gracious; a great lady of the old school, and she was pleased to twit me about my reluctance to admit that some day even *she* . . . ah, well, will-making is a painful matter; but I remember her, gallant as ever. . ."

"That's all rubbish, Farebrother," said Mr. Nutley rudely, as his partner showed signs of meandering indefinitely on; "gracious, indeed! When you know she terrified you nearly out of your life. You always get mawkish like this about people once they're dead."

Mr. Farebrother blinked mildly, and Nutley continued without taking any further notice of him.

"You haven't done so well out of this as John Fortune," he said to Stanforth, "and you'll have a deal more trouble."

"I take it," said Stanforth, getting up and striding about the room, "that in the matter of this estate there are a great many liabilities and no assets to speak of, except the estate itself? To start with, there's a twenty-thousand-pound mortgage. What's the income from the farms?"

"A bare two thousand a year."

"So you start the year with a deficit, having paid off your income tax and the interest on the mortgage. Disgusting," said Stanforth. "One thing, at any rate, is clear: the place must go. One could just manage to keep the house, of course, but I don't see how anyone could afford to live in it, having kept it. The land isn't worth over much, but luckily we've got the house and gardens. What figure, Nutley? Thirty thousand? Forty?"

Mr. Nutley whistled.

"You're optimistic. The house isn't so very large, and it's inconvenient, no bathrooms, no electric light, no garage, no central heating. The buyer would have all that on his hands, and the moat ought to be cleaned out too. It's insanitary."

"Still, the house is historical," said Stanforth; "I think we can safely say thirty thousand for the house. It's a perfect specimen of Elizabethan, so I've always been told, and has the Tudor moat and outbuildings into the bargain. Thirty thousand for the house," he noted on a piece of paper.

"I wouldn't care for it myself," said Mr. Nutley, looking round, "low rooms, dark passages, a stinking moat, and a slippery staircase. If that's Tudor, you're welcome to it." His voice had a peculiarly malignant intonation. "Still, it's a gentleman's place, I don't deny, and ought to make an interesting item under the hammer." He passed the tip of his tongue over his lips, a gesture horridly voluptuous in one so sharp and meagre.

"Then we have the furniture and the tapestries and the pictures," Stanforth went on. "I think we might reckon another twenty thousand for them. Americans, you know—or the buyer of the house might care for some of the furniture. The pictures aren't of much value, so I understand, save as of family interest. Twenty thousand. That clears off the mortgage. What about the farms and the land?"

"You could split some of the park up into building lots," said Mr. Nutley.

Mr. Farebrother gave a little exclamation.

"The park—it's a pretty park, Nutley."

"Very pretty, and any builder who chose to run up half a dozen villas would be a sensible chap," Mr. Nutley replied, wilfully misunderstanding him. "I should suggest a site at the top of the hill, where you get the view. What do you think, Colonel Stanforth?"

"I think the buyer of the house should be given the option of buying in the whole of the park, that section being reserved at the price of accommodation land, if he chooses to pay for it."

Mr. Nutley nodded. He approved of Colonel Stanforth as an adequately shrewd business man.

"There remain the farm lands," he said, referring to his papers. "Two thousand acres, roughly; three good farm houses; and a score of cottages. It's a little difficult to price. Say, taking one thing in with another, twenty pounds an acre, including the buildings—a good deal of the land is worthless. Forty thousand. We've disposed now of all the assets. We shall be lucky if we can clear the death-duties and mortgage out of the proceeds of the sale, and let Mr. Chase go with whatever amount the house itself fetches to bring him in a few hundreds a year for the rest of his life."

They stared across at Chase, whose concern with the affair they appeared hitherto to have forgotten. Mr. Farebrother alone kept his eyes bent down, as very meticulously he sharpened the point of his pencil.

"It's an unsatisfactory situation," said Mr. Nutley; "if I were Chase I should resent being dragged away from my ordinary business on such an unprofitable affair. He'll be lucky, as you say, if he clears the actual value of the house for himself after everything is settled up. Now, are we to try for auction or private treaty? Personally I think the house at any rate will go by private treaty. The present tenants will probably buy in their own farms. But the house, if it's reasonably well advertised, ought to attract a number of private buyers. We must have a decent caretaker to show people over the place. I suggest the present butler? He was in Miss Chase's service for thirty years." He looked round for approval; Chase and Stanforth both nodded, though Chase felt so much of an outsider that he wondered whether Nutley would consider him justified in nodding. "Ring the bell, Farebrother, will you? It's just behind you. Look at the bell, gentlemen! what an antiquated arrangement! There's no doubt, the house is terribly inconvenient."

Fortune, the butler, came in, a thin grizzled man in decent black.

Perhaps you had better give your instructions, Nutley, Chase said from the window-seat as the solicitor glanced at him with conventional hesitation.

"I'm speaking for Mr. Chase, Fortune," said Mr. Nutley. "Your late mistress's will unfortunately isn't very satisfactory, and Blackboys will be in the market before very long. We want you to stay on until then, with such help as you need, and you must tell the other servants they have all a month's notice. By the way, you inherit five hundred pounds under the will, but it'll be sometime before you get it."

"Blackboys in the market?" Fortune began.

"Oh, my good man, don't start lamenting again here," exclaimed Mr. Nutley hurriedly; "think of those five hundred pounds—a very nice little sum of which we should all be glad, I'm sure."

"Dear me, dear me," said Mr. Farebrother, much distressed, and he got up and patted Fortune on the shoulder.

Nutley was collecting the papers again into a neat packet, boxing them together on the table as though they had been a pack of cards. He glanced up to say,

"That settled, Fortune? Then we needn't keep you any longer; thanks. Well, Mr. Chase, if there's anything we can do for you tomorrow, you have only to ring me up or Farebrother—oh, I forgot, of course, you aren't on the telephone here."

Chase, who had been thinking to himself that Nutley was a splendid man—really efficient, a first-class man, was suddenly aware that he resented the implied criticism.

"I can go to the post-office if I want to telephone," he said coldly.

Mr. Farebrother noticed the coldness in his tone, and thought regretfully, "Dear me, Nutley has offended him—ignored him completely all the time. I ought to have put that right—very remiss of me."

He said aloud,

"If Mr. Chase would prefer not to sleep in the house, I should be very glad to offer him hospitality. . ."

"Afraid of the old lady's ghost, Chase?" said Mr. Nutley with a laugh that concealed a sneer.

They all laughed, with exception of Mr. Farebrother, who was pained.

Chase was tired; he wished they would go; he wanted to be alone.

II

He was alone; they had gone, Stanforth striding off across the park in his rather ostentatious suit of large checks and baggy knickerbockers, the two solicitors, with their black leather hand-bags, trundling down the avenue in the station cab. They had gone, they and their talk of mortgages, rents, acreage, tenants, possible buyers, building lots, and sales by auction or private treaty! Chase stood on the bridge above the moat, watching their departure. He was still a little confused in his mind, not having had time to turn round and think since Stanforth's telegram had summoned him that morning. Arrived at Blackboys, he had been immediately commandeered by Nutley, had had wishes and opinions put into his mouth, and had found a complete set of intentions ready-made for him to assume as his own. That had all saved him a lot of trouble, undoubtedly; but nevertheless he was glad of a breathing-space; there were things he wanted to think over; ideas he wanted to get used to. . .

He was poor; and hard-working in a cheerless fashion; he managed a branch of a small insurance company in Wolverhampton, and expected nothing further of life. Not very robust, his days in an office left him with little energy after he had conscientiously carried out his business. He lived in lodgings in Wolverhampton, smoking rather too much and eating rather too little. He had neither loved nor married. He had always known that some day, when his surviving aunt was dead, he would inherit Blackboys, but Blackboys was only a name to him, and he had gauged that the inheritance would mean for him nothing but trouble and interruption, and that once the whole affair was wound up he would resume his habitual existence just where he had dropped it.

His occupations and outlook might thus be comprehensively summarized.

He turned to look back at the house. Any man brighter-hearted and more optimistic might have rejoiced in this enforced expedition as a holiday, but Chase was neither optimistic nor bright-hearted. He took life with a dreary and rather petulant seriousness, and, full of resentment against this whole unprofitable errand, was dwelling now upon the probable, the almost certain, inefficiencies of his subordinates in Wolverhampton, because he had in him an old-maidish trait that could not endure the thought of other people interfering with his business or his possessions. He worried, in his small anæmic mind that was too restricted to be contemptuous, and too diffident to be really bad-tempered. . . The house looked down at him, grave and mellow. Its façade of old, plum-coloured bricks, the inverted V of the two gables, the rectangles of the windows, and the creamy stucco of the little colonnade that joined the two projecting wings, all reflected unbroken in the green stillness of the moat. It was not a large house; it consisted only of the two wings and the central block, but it was complete and perfect; so perfect, that Chase, who knew and cared nothing about architecture, and whose mind was really absent, worrying, in Wolverhampton, was gradually softened into a comfortable satisfaction. The house was indeed small, sweet, and satisfying. There was no fault to be found with the house. It was lovely in colour and design. It carried off, in its perfect proportions, the grandeur of its manner with an easy dignity. It was quiet, the evening was quiet, the country was quiet; it was part of the evening and the country. The country was almost unknown to Chase, whose life had been spent in towns—factory towns. Here he was on the borders of Kent and Sussex where the nearest town was a village, a jumble of cottages round a green, at his own park gates. The house seemed to lie at the very heart of peace.

A little wooden gate, moss-grown and slightly dilapidated, cut off the bridge from the gravelled entrance-space; he shut and latched it, and stood on the island that the moat surrounded. Swallows were swooping along the water, for the air was full of insects in the golden haze of the May evening. Faint clouds of haze hung about, blue and gold, deepening the mystery of the park, shrouding the recesses of the garden. The place was veiled. Chase put out his hand as though to push aside a veil. . .

He detected himself in the gesture, and glanced round guiltily to see whether he was observed. But he was alone; even the curtains behind the windows were drawn. He felt a desire to explore the garden, but hesitated, timorous and apologetic. Hitherto in his life he had explored only other people's gardens on the rare days when they were opened to the public; he remembered with what pained incredulity he had watched the public helping itself to the flowers out of the borders, for he could not help being a great respecter of property. He prided himself, of course, on being a Socialist; that was the fashion amongst the young men he occasionally frequented in Wolverhampton; but unlike them he was a Socialist whose sense of veneration was deeper and more instinctive than his socialism. He had thought at the time that he would be very indignant if he were the owner of the garden. Now that he actually was the owner, he hesitated before entering the garden, with a sense of intrusion. Had he caught sight of a servant he would certainly have turned and strolled off in the opposite direction.

The house lay in the hollow at the bottom of a ridge of wooded hills that sheltered it from the north, but the garden was upon the slope of the hill, in design quite simple: a central walk divided the square garden into halves, eased into very flat, shallow steps, and outlined by a low stone coping. A wall surrounded the whole garden. To reach the garden from the house, you crossed a little footbridge over the moat, at the bottom of the central walk. This simplicity, so obvious, yet, like the house, so satisfying, could not possibly have been otherwise ordered; it was married to the lie of the land. It flattered Chase with the delectable suggestion that he, a simple fellow, could have conceived and carried out the scheme as well as had the architect.

He was bound to admit that a simple fellow would not have thought of the peacocks. They were the royal touch that redeemed the gentle friendliness of the house and garden from all danger of complacency. He paused in amazement now at his first real sight of them. All the way up the low stone wall on either side of the central walk they sat, thirty or forty of them, their long tails sweeping down almost to the ground, the delicate crowns upon their heads erect in a feathery line of perspective, and the blue of their breasts rich above the grey stone coping. Half way up the walk, the coping was broken by two big stone balls, and upon one of these a peacock stood with his tail fully spread behind him, and uttered his discordant cry as though in the triumph and pride of his beauty.

Chase paused. He was too shy even to disturb those regal birds. He imagined the swirl of colour and the screech of indignation that would accompany his advance, and before their arrogance his timidity was abashed. But he stood there for a very long while, looking at them, until the garden became swathed in the shrouds of the blue evening, very dusky and venerable. He did not pass over the moat, but stood on the little bridge, between the house and the garden, while those shrouds of evening settled with the hush of vespers round him, and as he looked he kept saying to himself "Mine? *mine?*" in a puzzled and deprecatory way.

III

When Fortune showed him his room before dinner he was silent and inclined to scoff. He had been shown the other rooms by Nutley when he first arrived, and had gazed at them, accepting them without surprise, much as he would have gazed at rooms in some show-place or princely palace that he had paid a shilling to visit. The hall, the dining-room, the library, the long gallery—he had looked at them all, and had nodded in reply to the solicitor's comments, but not for a moment had it entered his head to regard the rooms as his own. To be left, however, in this room that resembled all the others, and to be told that it was his bedroom; to realize that he was to sleep inside that brocaded four-poster with the ostrich plumes nodding on the top; to envisage the trivial and vulgar functions of his daily dressing and undressing as taking place within this room that although so small was yet so stately—this was a shock that made him draw in his breath. Left alone, his hand raised to give a tug at his tie, he stared round and emitted a soft whistle. The walls were hung with tapestry, a grey-green landscape of tapestry, the borders formed by two fat twisted columns, looped across with garlands of flowers and fruits, and cherubs with distended cheeks blew zephyrs across this woven Arcady. High-backed Stuart chairs of black and gold. . . Chase wanted to take off his boots, but did not venture to sit down on the tawny cane-work. He moved about gingerly, afraid of spoiling something. Then he remembered that everything was his to spoil if he so chose. Everything waited on his good pleasure; the whole house, all those rooms, the garden; all those unknown farms and acres that Nutley and Stanforth had discussed. The thought produced no exhilaration in him, but, rather, an extreme embarrassment and alarm. He was more than ever dismayed to think that someone, sooner or later, was certain to come to him for orders. . .

He hesitated for an appreciable time before making up his mind to go down to dinner; in fact, even after he had resolutely pushed open his bedroom door, he still wavered upon its threshold. The landing, lit by the yellow flame of a solitary candle stuck into a silver sconce, was full of shadows: the well of the staircase gaped black; and across the great window red velvet curtains had been drawn, and now hung from floor to ceiling. Down the passage, behind one of those mysterious closed doors, lay the old woman dead in her pompous bed. So the house must have drowsed, evening after evening, before Chase ever came near it, with the only difference that from one of those doors had emerged an old lady dressed in black silk, leaning on a stick, an arbitrary old lady, who had slowly descended the polished stairs, carefully placing the rubber ferule of her stick from step to step, and helping herself on the banisters with the other hand, instead of the alien clerk from Wolverhampton, who hesitated to go downstairs to dinner because he feared there would be a servant in the room to wait upon him.

There was. Chase dined miserably, and was relieved only when he was left alone, port and madeira set before him, and the four candles reflected in the shining oak table. A greyhound, which had joined him at the foot of the stairs, now sat gravely beside him, and he gave him bits of biscuit as he had not dared to do in the presence of the servant. More at his ease at last, he sat thinking what he would do with the few hundreds a year Nutley predicted for him. Not such an unprofitable business after all, perhaps! He would be able to move from his lodgings in Wolverhampton; perhaps he could take a small villa with a little bit of garden in front. His imagination did not extend beyond Wolverhampton. Perhaps he could keep back one or two pieces of plate from the sale; he would like to have something to remind him of his connection with Blackboys and with his family. He cautiously picked up a porringer that was the only ornament on the table, and examined it. It gave him a little shock of familiarity to see that the coat-of-arms engraved on it was the same as the coat on his own signet ring, inherited from his father, and the motto was the same too: *Intabescantque Relictâ*, and the tiny peregrine falcon as the crest. Absurd to be surprised! He ought to remember that he wasn't a stranger here; he was Chase, no less than the old lady had been Chase, no less than all the portraits upstairs were Chase. He had already seen that coat-of-arms today, in the heraldic window, but without taking in its meaning. It gave him a new sense of confidence now, reassuring him that he wasn't the interloper he felt himself to be.

It was pleasant enough to linger here, with silence and shadows all round the pool of candlelight, that lit the polish of the table, the curves of the silver, and the dark wine in the round-bellied decanters; pleasant to dream of that villa which might now be attainable; but he had better go, or the servant would be coming to clear away.

Rising, he went out into the hall, followed by the dog, who seemed to have adopted him unquestioningly. As Chase didn't know his name, he bent down to read the inscription on the collar, but found only the address: CHASE, BLACKBOYS. That had been the old lady's address, of course, but it would do for him too; he needn't have the collar altered. CHASE, BLACKBOYS. It was simply handed on; no change. It gave him a queer sensation; this coming to Blackboys was certainly a queer experience, interrupting his life. He scarcely knew where he was as yet, or what he was doing; he had to keep reminding himself with an effort.

In the hall he hesitated, uncertain as to which was the door of the library, afraid that if he opened the wrong door he would find himself in the servants' quarters, perhaps even open it on them as they sat at supper. The dog stood in front of one door, wagging his tail and looking up at Chase, so he tried the handle; it was the wrong door, but instead of leading to the servants' quarters it opened straight on to the moonlit garden. The greyhound bounded out and ran about in the moonlight, a wraith of a dog in the ghostly garden. Ghostly. . . Chase wandered out, up the walk to the top of the garden, where he turned to look down upon the house, folded black in the hollow, the moonlight gleaming along the moat and winking on a window. Not a breath ruffled that milky stillness; the great cloths of light lay spread out over the grass, the blocks of shadow were profound; above the low-lying park trailed a faint white mist, and in a vaporous sky the moon rode calm and sovereign. Chase felt that on a scene so perfectly set something ought to happen. A pity that it should all be wasted. . . How many such nights must have been wasted! the prodigal loveliness of summer nights, lying illusory under the moon, shamelessly soliciting romance! But nothing happened; there was nothing but Chase looking down on the silent house, looking for a long time down on the silent house, and thinking that, on that night so set for a lovers' meeting, no lovers had met.

IV

He was very glad when the funeral was over, and he was rid of all the strange neighbours who had wrung his hand and uttered commiserating phrases. He was also glad that the house should be relieved of the presence of his aunt, for he could tread henceforth unrestrained by the idea that the corpse might rise up and with a pointing finger denounce his few and timorous orders. He stood now on the threshold of the library downstairs, looking at a bowl of coral-coloured tulips whose transparent delicacy detached itself brightly in the sober panelled room. He was grateful to the quietness that slumbered always over the house, abolishing fret as by a calm rebuke.

His recollections of the funeral were, he found to his dismay, principally absurd. Mr. Farebrother had sidled up to him, when he thought Nutley was preoccupied elsewhere, as they returned on foot up the avenue after the ceremony. "A great pity the place should have to go," Mr. Farebrother had said, trotting along beside him, "such a very great pity." Chase had agreed in a perfunctory way. "Perhaps it won't come to that," said Mr. Farebrother with a vague hopefulness. Chase again murmured something in the nature of agreement. "I like to think things will come right until the moment they actually go wrong," Mr. Farebrother said with a smile. "Very sad, too, the death of your aunt," he added. "Yes," said Chase. "Well, well, perhaps it isn't so bad as we think," said Mr. Farebrother, causing Chase to stare at him, thoroughly startled this time by the extent of the rosy old man's optimism.

But he was not now dwelling upon the funeral. Tomorrow he must leave Blackboys. No doubt he would find his affairs in Wolverhampton in a terrible way. He said to himself, "Tut-tut," his mind absent, though his eyes were still upon the tulips; but his annoyance over the office in Wolverhampton was largely superficial. Business had a claim on him, certainly; the business of his employers; but his own private business had a claim too, that, moreover, would take up but a month or two out of his life; after that Blackboys would be sold, and would engage no more of his time away from Wolverhampton. Blackboys would pass to other hands, making no further demands upon Peregrine Chase. It would be a queer little incident to look back upon; his few acquaintances in Wolverhampton, with whom he sometimes played billiards of an evening, or joined in a whist drive, would stare, derisive and incredulous, if the story ever leaked out, at the idea of Chase as a landed proprietor. As a squire! As the descendant of twenty generations! Why, no one in Wolverhampton knew so much as his Christian name; he had been careful always to sign his letters with a discreet initial, so that if they thought of it at all they probably thought him Percy. A friend would have nosed it out. There was a safeguard in friendlessness. Chase was a reticent little man, as his solicitors had had occasion to remark. Nutley found this very convenient: Chase, making no comment, left him free to manage everything according to his own ideas. Indeed, Nutley frequently forgot his very existence. It was most convenient.

As for Chase, he wondered sometimes absently which he disliked least: Farebrother with his weak sentimentality, or Nutley, who was so astute, so bent upon getting Blackboys brilliantly into the market, and whose grudging respect for old Miss Chase, beneath his impatience of the tyranny she had imposed upon him, was so readily divined.

Chase stood looking at the bowl of tulips; it seemed to him that he spent his days forever looking at something, and deriving from it that new, quiet satisfaction. He was revolving in his mind a phrase of Mr. Farebrother's, to the effect that he ought to go the rounds and call upon his tenants. "They'll expect it, you know," Farebrother had said, examining Chase over the top of his spectacles. Chase had gone through a moment of panic, until he remembered that his departure on the morrow would postpone this ordeal. But it remained uncomfortably with him. He had seen his tenants at the funeral, and had eyed them surreptitiously when he thought they were not noticing him. They were all farmers, big, heavy, kindly men, whose manner had adopted little Chase into the shelter of an interested benevolence. He had liked them; distinctly he had liked them. But to call upon them in their homes, to intrude upon their privacy—he who of all men had a wilting horror of intrusion, that was another matter.

He enjoyed being alone himself; he had a real taste for solitude, and luxuriated now in his days and particularly his evenings at Blackboys, when he sat over the fire, stirring the great heap of soft grey ashes with the poker, the ashes that were never cleared away; he liked the woolly thud when the poker dropped among them. Those evenings were pleasant to him; pleasant and new, though sometimes he felt that in spite of their novelty they had been always a part of his life. Moreover he had a companion, for Thane, the greyhound, slim and fawn-coloured, lay by the fire asleep, with his nose along his paws.

There existed in his mind a curious confusion in regard to his tenants, a confusion quite childish, but which carried with it a sort of terror. It dated from the day when, for want of something better to do, he had turned over some legal papers left behind by Nutley, and the dignity of his manor had disclosed itself to him in all the brocaded stiffness of its ancient ritual and phraseology. He had laughed; he could not help laughing; but he had been impressed and even a little awed. The weight of legend seemed to lie suddenly heavy upon his shoulders, and he had gazed at his own hands, as though he expected to see them mysteriously loaded with rough hierarchical rings. Vested in him, all this antiquity and surviving ceremonial! He read again the almost incomprehensible words that had first caught his eye, scraps here and there as he turned the pages. "There are three teams in demesne, 31 villains, with 14 bordars, i.e., the class who should not pay live heriot. The furrow-long measures 40 roods, i.e., 40 lengths of the Ox-goad of 16½ feet, a rod just long enough to lie along the yokes of the first three pair of Oxen, and let the ploughman thrust with the point at either flank of either the sod ox or the sward ox. Such a strip four rods in width gives an acre." "There is wood of 75 Hogs. The Hogs must be panage Hogs, one in seven, paid each year for the right to feed the herd in the Lord of the Manor's wooded wastes."

What on earth were panage hogs, to which apparently he was entitled?

He read again, "The quantum of liberty of person and alienation originally enjoyed by those now represented by the Free Tenants of the Manor is a matter of argument for the theorists. The free tenants were *liberi homines* within the statute *Quia Emptores Terrarum*, and as such from 1289 could sell their holdings to whomsoever they would, without the Lord's licence, still less without surrender or admittance, saving always the condition that the feoffee do hold of the same Lord as feoffor. And the feoffee must hold, i.e., must acknowledge that he hold. There must be a tenure in fact and the Lord must know his new tenant as such. Some privity must be established. The new tenant must do fealty and say 'I hold of you, the Lord.' An alienation without such acknowledgement is not good against the Lord."

He laid down the papers. Could such things be actualities? This must be the copy of some old record he had got hold of. But no; he turned back to the first page and found the date of the previous year. It appalled him to think that since such things had happened to his aunt, they were also liable to happen to him. What would he do with a panage hog, supposing one were driven up to the front door? Still less would he know what to do if one of those farmers he had seen at the funeral were to say to him, "I hold of you, the Lord."

Then he remembered that he had not found the people in the village alarming. He remembered a conversation he had had the day before, with a man and his wife, as he leaned over the gate that led into their little garden. On either side of the tiled path running up to the cottage door were broad beds filled with a jumble of flowers—pansies, lupins, tulips, honesty, sweet-rocket, and bright fragile poppies.

"Lovely show of flowers you have there," he had said tentatively to a woman in an apron, who stood inside the gate knitting.

"It's like that all the summer," she replied, "my husband's very proud of his garden, he is. But we're under notice to quit." She spoke with an unfamiliar broad accent and a burr, that had prompted Chase to say,

"You're not from these parts?"

"No, sir, I'm from Sussex. It's not a wonderful great matter of distance. I'm wanting my man to come back with me, and settle near my old home, but he says he was born in Kent and in Kent he'll die."

"That's right," approved the man who had come up. "I don't hold with folk leaving their own county. It's like sheep—take sheep away from their own parts, and they don't do near so well. Oxfordshire don't do on Romney Marsh, and Romney Marsh don't do in Oxfordshire." He was ramming tobacco into his pipe, but broke off to pull a seedling of groundsel out from among his pinks. He crushed it together and put it carefully into his pocket. "I made this garden," he resumed, "carried the mould home on my back evening after evening, and sent the kids out with bodges for road-scrapings, till you couldn't beat my soil, sir, not in this village, nor my flowers either. But I'm under notice, and sooner than let them pass to a stranger I'll put my bagginhook through the roots of every plant amongst them," he said, and spat.

"Twenty-five years we've lived in this cottage, and brought up ten children," said the woman.

"The cottage is to come down, and make room for a building site, so Mr. Nutley told us," the man continued.

"We'd papered and whitewashed it ourselves," said the woman.

"I laid them tiles, sir, me and my eldest boy," said the man, pointing with the stem of his pipe down at the path; "a rare job it was. There wasn't no garden, not when I came here."

"Twenty-five years ago," said the woman.

They both stared mournfully at Chase.

"I'm under notice to quit, too, you know," said Chase, rather embarrassed, as though they had brought a gentle reproof against him, trying to excuse himself by this joke.

"I know that, sir; we're sorry," the man had said instantly.

(Sorry. They had never seen him before, yet they were sorry.)

"Miss Chase, your aunt, sir, liked my garden properly," said the man. "She'd stop here always, in her pony-chaise, and have a look at my flowers. She'd say to me, chaffing-like, 'You've a better show than me, Jakes.' But she didn't like peonies. I had a fine clump of peonies and she made me dig it up. Lord, she was a tartar—saving your presence, sir. But a good heart, so nobody took no notice. But peonies—no, she wouldn't have peonies at any price."

"There's few folks in this village ever thought to see Blackboys in other hands than Chase's," said the woman. "'Tis the peacocks will be grieved—dear! dear!"

"The peacocks?" Chase had repeated.

"Folks about here do say, the peacocks'll die off when Blackboys goes from Chase's hands," said the man. "They be terrible hard on a garden, though, do be peacocks," he had said further, meticulously removing another weed from among his pinks.

V

That had been an experience to Chase, a milestone on his road. He was to experience much the same sensation when his lands received him. It was a new world to him—new because it was so old—ancient and sober according to the laws of nature. There was here a rhythm which no flurry could disturb. The seasons ordained, and men lived close up against the rulings so prescribed, close up against the austere laws, at once the masters and the subjects of the land that served them and that they as loyally served. Chase perceived his mistake; he perceived it with surprise and a certain reverence. Because the laws were unalterable they were not necessarily stagnant. They were of a solemn order, not arbitrarily framed or admitting of variation according to the caprice of mankind. In the place of stagnation, he recognized stability. And as his vision widened he saw that the house fused very graciously with the trees, the meadows, and the hills, grown there in place no less than they, a part of the secular tradition. He reconsidered even the pictures, not as the representation of meaningless ghosts, but as men and women whose blood had gone to the making of that now in his own veins. It was the land, the farms, the rickyards, the sown, the fallow, that taught him this wisdom. He learnt it slowly, and without knowing that he learnt. He absorbed it in the company of men such he had never previously known, and who treated him as he had never before been treated—not with deference only, which would have confused him, but with a paternal kindliness, a quiet familiarity, an acquaintance immediately linked by virtue of tradition. To them he, the clerk of Wolverhampton, was, quite simply, Chase of Blackboys. He came to value the smile in their eyes, when they looked at him, as a caress.

VI

When Nutley came again, a fortnight after the funeral, to his surprise he met Chase in the park with Thane, the greyhound, at his heels.

"Good gracious," he said, "I thought you were in Wolverhampton?"

"So I was. I thought I'd come back to see how things were going on. I arrived two days ago."

"But I saw Fortune last week, and he never mentioned your coming," pursued Mr. Nutley, mystified.

"No, I daresay he didn't; in point of fact, he knew nothing about it until I turned up here."

"What, you didn't let the servants know?"

"No, I didn't," Chase entered suddenly upon a definite dislike of Mr. Nutley. He felt a relief as soon as he had realized it; he felt more settled and definite in his mind, cleared of the cobwebs of a vague uneasiness. Nutley was too inquisitorial, too managing altogether. Blackboys was his own to come to, if he chose. Still his own—for another month.

"What on earth have you got there?" said Nutley peering at a crumpled bunch that Chase carried in his hand.

"Butcher-boys," replied Chase.

"They're wild orchids," said Mr. Nutley, after peering a little closer. "Why do you call them butcher-boys?"

"That's what the children call them," mumbled Chase, "I don't know them by any other name. Ugly things, anyhow," he added, flinging them violently away.

"Soft, soft," said Nutley to himself, tapping his forehead as he walked on alone.

He proceeded towards the house. Queer of Chase, to come back like that, without a word to anyone. What about that business of his in Wolverhampton? He seemed to be less anxious about that now. As though he couldn't leave matters to Nutley and Farebrother, Solicitors and Estate Agents, without slipping back to see to things himself! Spying, no less. Queer, sly, silent fellow, mooning about the park, carrying wild orchids. "Butcher-boys," he had called them. What children had he been consorting with, to learn that country name? There had been an odd look in his eye, too, when Nutley had come upon him, as though he were vexed at being seen, and would have liked to slink off in the opposite direction. Queer, too, that he should have made no reference to the approaching sale. He might at least have asked whether the estate office had received any private applications. But Nutley had already noticed that he took very little interest in the subject of the sale. An unsatisfactory employer, except in so far as he never interfered; it was unsatisfactory never to know whether one's employer approved of what was being done or not.

And under his irritability was another grievance: the suspicion that Chase was a dark horse. The solicitor had always marked down Blackboys as a ripe plum to fall into his hands when old Miss Chase died—obstinate, opinionated, old Phillida Chase. He had never considered the heir at all. It was almost as though he looked upon himself as the heir—the impatient heir, hostile and vindictive towards the coveted inheritance.

Nutley reached the house, where, his hand upon the latch of the little wooden gate, he was checked by a padlock within the hasp. He was irritated, and shook the latch roughly. He thought that the quiet house, safe behind its gate and its sleeping moat, smiled and mocked him. Then, more sensibly, he pulled the bell beside the gate, and waited till the tinkle inside the house brought Fortune hurrying to open.

"What's this affair, eh, Fortune?" said Nutley with false good-humour, pointing to the padlock.

"The padlock, sir? That's there by Mr. Chase's orders," replied Fortune demurely.

"Mr. Chase's orders?" repeated Mr. Nutley, not believing his own ears.

"Mr. Chase has been very much annoyed, sir, by motoring parties coming to look over the house, and making free of the place."

"But they may have been intending purchasers!" Mr. Nutley almost shrieked, touched upon the raw.

"Yes, sir, they all had orders to view. All except one party, that is, that came yesterday. Mr. Chase turned *them* away, sir."

"Turned them away?"

"Yes, sir. They came in a big car. Mr. Chase talked to them himself, through the gate. He had the key in his pocket. No, sir, he wouldn't unlock it. He said that if they wanted to buy the house they would have the opportunity of doing so at the auction. Yes, sir, they seemed considerably annoyed. They said they had come from London on purpose. They said they should have thought that if anyone had a house to sell, he would have been only too glad to show parties over it, order or no order. They said, especially if the house was so unsaleable, two hours by train from London and not up to date in anyway. Mr. Chase said, very curt-like, that if they wanted an up-to-date house, Blackboys was not likely to suit them. He just lifted his cap, and wished them good-evening, and came back by himself into the house, with the key still in his pocket, and the car drove away. Very insolent sort of people they were, sir, I must say."

Fortune delivered himself of this recital in a tone that was a strange compound of respect, reticence, and a secret relish. During its telling he had followed Mr. Nutley's attentive progress into the house, until they arrived in the panelled library where the coral-coloured tulips reared themselves so luminously against the sobriety of the books and of the oak. Mr. Nutley noticed them, because it was easier to pass a comment on a bowl of flowers than upon Chase's inexplicable behaviour.

"Yes, sir, very pretty; Mr. Chase puts them there," said Fortune, with the satisfaction of one who adds a final touch to a suggestive sketch.

"Shouldn't have thought he'd ever looked at a flower in his life," muttered Nutley.

He deposited his bag on the table, and turned to the butler.

"Quite between you and me, Fortune, what you tell me surprises me very much—about the visiting parties, I mean. And the padlock. Um— the padlock. I always thought Mr. Chase very *quiet*; but you don't, do you, think him *soft*?"

Fortune knew that Nutley enjoyed saying that. He remembered how he had caught Chase, the day before, studying bumbledories on the low garden wall; but he withheld the bumbledories from Mr. Nutley.

"It wouldn't be unnatural, sir," he submitted, "if Mr. Chase had a feeling about Blackboys being in the market?"

"Feeling? pooh!" said Mr. Nutley. He said "Pooh!" again to reassure himself, because he knew that Fortune, stupid, sentimental, and shrewd, had hit the nail on the head. "He'd never set eyes on Blackboys until three weeks ago. Besides, what could he do with the place except put it in the market? Tell me that? Absurd!"

He was sorting papers out of his black bag. Their neat stiffness gave him the reassuring sense of being here among matters which he competently understood. This was his province. He would have said, had he been asked a day earlier, that it was Chase's province too. Now he was not so sure.

"Sentimentality!" he snorted. It was his most damning criticism.

Chase's pipe was lying on the table beside the tulips; he picked it up and regarded it with a mixture of reproach and indignation. It reposed mutely in his hand.

"Ridiculous!" said Nutley, dashing it down again as though that settled the matter.

"The people round here have taken to him wonderful," put in Fortune.

Nutley looked sharply at him; he stood by the table, demure, grizzled, and perfectly respectful.

"Why, has he been round talking to the people?"

"A good deal, sir, among the tenants like. Wonderful how he gets on with them, for a city-bred man. I don't hold with city-breeding, myself. Will you be staying to luncheon, sir?"

"Yes," replied Mr. Nutley, preoccupied and profoundly suspicious.

VII

Suspicious of Chase, though he couldn't justify his suspicion. Tested even by the severity of the solicitor's standards, Chase's behaviour and conversation during luncheon were irreproachable. No sooner had he entered the house than he began briskly talking of business. Yet Nutley continued to eye him as one who beneath reasonable words and a bland demeanour nourishes a secret and a joke; a silent and deeply-buried understanding. He talked sedately enough, keeping to the subject even with a certain rigour—acreage, rents, building possibilities; an intelligent interest. Still, Nutley could have sworn there was irony in it. Irony from Chase? Weedy, irritable little man, Chase. Not today, though; not irritable today. In a good temper. (Ironical?) Playing the host, sitting at the head of the refectory-table while Nutley sat at the side. Naturally. Very cordial, very open-handed with the port. Quite at home in the dining-room, ordering his dog to a corner; and in the library too, with his pipes and tobacco strewn about. How long ago was it, since Nutley was warning him not to slip on the polished boards?

Then a stroll round the garden, Chase with crumbs in his pocket for the peacocks. When they saw him, two or three hopped majestically down from the parapet, and came stalking towards him. Accustomed to crumbs evidently. "You haven't had them destroyed, then?" said Nutley, eyeing them with mistrust and disapproval, and Chase laughed without answering. Up the centre walk of the garden, and back by the herbaceous borders along the walls: lilac, wistaria, patches of tulips, colonies of iris. All the while Chase never deviated from the topic of selling. He pointed out the house, folded in the hollow down the gentle slope of the garden. "Not bad, for those who like it. Thirty thousand for the house, I think you said?" "Then why the devil," Nutley wanted to say, but refrained from saying, "do you turn away people who come in a big car?" They strolled down the slope, Chase breaking from the lilac bushes an armful of the heavy plumes. He seemed to do it with an unknowing gesture, as though he couldn't keep his hands off flowers, and then to be embarrassed on discovering in his arms the wealth that he had gathered. It was as though he had kept an adequate guard over his tongue while allowing his gestures to escape him. He took Nutley round to the entrance, where the station cab was waiting, and unlocked the gate with the key he carried in his pocket.

"You go back to Wolverhampton tomorrow?" said Mr. Nutley, preparing to depart.

"That's it," replied Chase. Did he look sly, or didn't he?

"All the arrangements will be made by the end of next week," said Nutley severely.

"That's splendid!" replied Chase.

Nutley, as he was driven away, had a last glimpse of him, leaning still against the gatepost, vaguely holding the lilac.

VIII

C hase didn't go back to Wolverhampton. He knew that it was his duty to go, but he stayed on at Blackboys. Not only that, but he sent no letter or telegram in explanation of his continued absence. He simply stayed where he was, callous, and supremely happy. By no logic could he have justified his behaviour; by no effort of the imagination could he, a fortnight earlier, have conceived such behaviour as proceeding from his well-ordered creeds. He stayed on, through the early summer days that throughout all their hours preserved the clarity of dawn. Like a child strayed into the realms of delight, he was stupefied by the enchantment of sun and shadow. He remained for hours gazing in a silly beatitude at the large patches of sunlight that lay on the grass, at the depths of the shadows that melted into the profundity of the woods. In the mornings he woke early, and leaning at the open window gave himself over to the dews, to the young glinting sunshine, and to the birds. What a babble of birds! He couldn't distinguish their notes—only to the cuckoo, the wood-pigeon, and the distant crow of a cock could he put a name. The fluffy tits, blue and yellow, hopping among the apple-branches, were to him as nameless as they were lovely. He knew, theoretically, that the birds did sing when day was breaking; the marvellous thing was, not that they should be singing, but that he, Chase, should be awake and in the country to hear them sing. No one knew that he was awake, and he had all a shy man's pleasure in seclusion. No one knew what he was doing; no one was spying on him; he was quite free and unobserved in this clean-washed, untenanted, waking world. Down in the woods only the small animals and the birds were stirring. There was the rustle of a mouse under dead leaves. It was too early for even the farm-people to be about. Chase and the natural citizens between them had it all their own way. (Nutley wore a black coat and carried a black shiny bag, but Nutley knew nothing of the dawn.) Then he clothed himself, and, passing out of the house unperceived with Thane, since there was no one to perceive them, wandered in the sparkling fields. There was by now no angle from which he was not familiar with the house, whether he considered the dreamy roofs from the crest of the hill or the huddle of the murrey-coloured buildings from across the distance of the surrounding pastures. No thread of smoke rose slim and wavering from a chimney but he could trace it down to its hearthstone. No window glittered but he could name the room it lit. Nor was there any tenderness of light whose change he had not observed, whether of the morning, cool and fluty; or of the richer evening, profound and venerable, that sank upon the ruby brick-work, the glaucous moat, and the breasts of the peacocks in the garden; or of the ethereal moonlight, a secret that he kept, inviolate almost from himself, in the shyest recesses of his soul.

For at the centre of all was always the house, that mothered the farms and accepted the homage of the garden. The house was at the heart of all things; the cycle of husbandry might revolve—tillage to growth, and growth to harvest—more necessary, more permanent, perhaps, more urgent; but like a woman gracious, humorous, and dominant, the house remained quiet at the centre. To part the house and the lands, or to consider them as separate, would be no less than parting the soul and the body. The house was the soul; did contain and guard the soul as in a casket; the lands were England, Saxon as they could be, and if the house were at the heart of the land, then the soul of the house must indeed be at the heart and root of England, and, once arrived at the soul of the house, you might fairly claim to have pierced to the soul of England. Grave, gentle, encrusted with tradition, embossed with legend, simple and proud, ample and maternal. Not sensational. Not arresting. There was nothing about the house or the country to startle; it was, rather, a charm that enticed, insidious as a track through a wood, or a path lying across fields and curving away from sight over the skyline, leading the unwary wanderer deeper and deeper into the bosom of the country.

He knew the sharp smell of cut grass, and the wash of the dew round his ankles. He knew the honing of a scythe, the clang of a forge and the roaring of its bellows, the rasp of a saw cutting through wood and the resinous scent of the sawdust. He knew the tap of a woodpecker on a tree-trunk, and the midday murmur, most amorous, most sleepy, of the pigeons among the beeches. He knew the contented buzz of a bee as it closed down upon a flower, and the bitter shrill of the grasshopper along the hedgerows. He knew the squirt of milk jetting into the pails, and the drowsy stir in the byres. He knew the marvellous brilliance of a petal in the sun, its fibrous transparency, like the cornelian-coloured transparency of a woman's fingers held over a strong light. He associated these sights, and the infinitesimal small sounds composing the recurrent melody, with the meals prepared for him, the salads and cold chicken, the draughts of cider, and abundance of fresh humble fruit, until it seemed to him that all senses were gratified severally and harmoniously, as well out in the open as in the cool dusk within the house.

He liked to rap with his stick upon the door of a farm-house, and to be admitted with a "Why! Mr. Chase!" by a smiling woman into the passage, smelling of recent soap and water on the tiles; to be ushered into the sitting-room, hideous, pretentious, and strangely meaningless, furnished always with the cottage-piano, the Turkey carpet, and the plant in a bright gilt basket-pot. The light in these rooms always struck Chase as being particularly unmerciful. But he learnt that he must sit patient, while the farmer was summoned, and the rest of the household too, and sherry in a decanter and a couple of glasses were produced from a sideboard, at whatever hour Chase's visit might chance to fall, be it even at eight in the morning, which it very often was. That lusty hospitality permitted no refusal of the sherry, though Chase might have preferred, instead of the burning stuff, a glass of fresh milk after his walk across the dews. He must sit and sip the sherry, responding to the social efforts of the farmer's wife and daughters (the latter always coy, always would be up to date), while the farmer was content to leave this indoor portion of the entertainment to his womenfolk, contributing nothing himself but "Another glass, Mr. Chase?" or the offer of a cigar, and the creak of his leather gaiters as he trod across the room. But presently, Chase knew, when the conversation became really impossibly stilted, he might without incivility suggest that he mustn't keep the farmer any longer from his daily business, and, after shaking hands all round with the ladies, might take his cap and follow his host out into the yard, where men pitchforked the sodden litter out into the midden in the centre of the yard, and the slow cattle lurched one behind the other from the sheds, turning themselves unprompted in the familiar direction. Here, Chase might be certain he would not be embarrassed by having undue notice taken of him. The farmer here was a greater man than he. Chase liked to follow round meekly, and the more he was neglected the better he was pleased. Then he and the farmer together would tramp across the acres, silent for the most part, but inwardly contented, although when the farmer broke the silence it was only to grunt out some phrase of complaint, either at the poverty of that year's yield, or the dearth or abundance of rabbits, or to remark, kicking at a clod of loam, "Soggy! soggy! the land's not yet forgotten the rains we had in February," thus endowing the land with a personality actual and rancorous, more definite to Chase than the personalities of the yeomen, whom he could distinguish apart by their appearance perhaps, but certainly not by their opinions, their preoccupations, or their gestures. They were natural features rather than men—trees or boles, endowed with speech and movement indeed, but preserving the same unity, the same hodden unwieldiness, that was integral with the landscape. There was one old hedger in particular who, maundering over his business of lop and top, or grubbing among the ditches, had grown as gnarled and horny as an ancient root, and was scarcely distinguishable till you came right upon him, when his little brown dog flew out from the hedge and barked; and there was another chubby old man, a dealer in fruit, who drove about the country, a long ladder swaying out of the back of his cart. This old man was intimate with every orchard of the country-side, whether apple, cherry, damson, or plum, and could tell you the harvest gathered in bushel measures for any year within his memory; but although all fruits came within his province, the apples had his especial affection, and he never referred to them save by the personal pronouns, "Ah, Winter Queening," he would say, "she's a grand bearer," or "King of the Pippins, he's a fine fellow," and for Chase, whom he had taken under his protection, he would always produce some choice specimen from his pocket with a confidential air, although, as he never failed to observe, "May wasn't the time for apples." Let Mr. Chase only wait till the autumn—he would show him what a Ribston or a Blenheim ought to be; "But I shan't be here in the autumn, Caleb," Chase would say, and the old man would jerk his head sagely and reply as he whipped up the pony, "Trees with old roots isn't so easily thrown over," and in the parable that he only half understood Chase found an obscure comfort.

These were his lane-made friendships. He knew the man who cut withes by the brook; he knew the gang and the six great shining horses that dragged away the chained and fallen trees upon an enormous wain; he knew the boys who went after moorhen's eggs; he knew the kingfisher that was always ambushed somewhere near the bridge; he knew the cheery woman who had an idiot child, and a husband accursed of bees. "Bees? no, my husband couldn't never go near bees. He squashed up too many of them when he was a lad, and bees never forget. Squashed 'em up, *so*, in his hand. Just temper. Now if three bees stung him together he'd die. Oh, surely, Mr. Chase, sir. We went down into Sussex once, on a holiday, and the bees there knew him at once and were after him.

Wonderful thing it is, the sense beasts have got. And memory! Beasts never forget, beasts don't."

And always there was the reference to the sale, and the regrets, that were never impertinent and never ruffled so much as the fringes of Chase's pride. The women were readier with these regrets than the men; they started off with unthinking sympathy, while the men shuffled and coughed, and traced with their toe the pattern of the carpet, but presently, when alone with Chase, took advantage of the women's prerogative in breaking the ice, to revive the subject; and always Chase, to get himself out of a conversation which he felt to be fraught with awkwardness—the awkwardness of reserved men trespassing upon the grounds of secret and personal feeling—would parry with his piteous jest of being himself under notice to quit.

IX

When the inventory men came, Chase suffered. They came with bags, ledgers, pencils; they were brisk and efficient, and Chase fled them from room to room. They soon put him down as oddly peevish, not knowing that they had committed the extreme offence of disturbing his dear privacy. In their eyes, after all, they were there as his employees, carrying out his orders. The foreman even went out of his way to be appreciative, "Nice lot of stuff you have there, sir," he said to Chase, when his glance first travelled over the dim velvets and gilt of the furniture in the Long Gallery; "should do well under the hammer." Chase stood beside him, seeing the upholstered depths of velvets and damasks, like ripe fruits, heavily fringed and tasselled; the plasterwork of the diapered ceiling; the fairy-tale background of the tapestry, and the reflections of the cloudy mirrors. Into this room also he had put bowls of flowers, not knowing that the inventory men were coming so soon. "Nice lot of stuff you have here, sir," said the foreman.

Chase remembered how often, representing his insurance company, he had run a casual and assessing eye over other people's possessions.

The inventory men worked methodically through the house. Ground floor, staircase, landing, passage, first floor. Everything was ticketed and checked. Chase miserably avoided their hearty communicativeness. He skulked in the sitting-room downstairs, or, when he was driven out of that, took his cap and walked away from the house that surrounded him now with the grief of a wistful reproach. He knew that he would be well-advised to leave, yet he delayed from day today; he suffered, but he stayed on, impotently watching the humbling and the desecration of the house. Then he took to going amongst the men when they were at their work, "What might be the value of a thing like this?" he would ask, tapping picture, cabinet, or chair with a contemptuous finger; and, when told, he would express surprise that anyone could be fool enough to pay such a price for an object so unserviceable, worm-eaten, or insecure. He would stand by, derisively sucking the top of his cane, while clerk and foreman checked and inscribed. Sometimes he would pick up some object just entered, a blue porcelain bowl, or whatever it might be, turn it over between his hands, examine it, and set it back on the window ledge with a shrug of the shoulders. There were no flowers in the rooms now, nor did he leave his pipes and tobacco littering the tables, but kept them hidden away in a drawer. There had been places, intimate to him, where he had grown accustomed to put his things, knowing he would find them there on his return; but he now broke himself of this weakness with a wrench. It hurt, and he was grim about it. In the evenings he sat solitary in a stiff room, without the companionship of those familiar things in their familiar niches. Towards Fortune his manner changed, and he appeared to take a pleasure in speaking callously, even harshly, of the forthcoming sale; but the old servant saw through him. When people came now to visit the house, he took them over every corner of it himself, deploring its lack of convenience, pointing out the easy remedy, and vaunting the advantage of its architectural perfection, "Quoted in every book on the subject," he would say, "a perfect specimen of domestic Elizabethan" (this phrase he had picked up from an article in an architectural journal), "complete in every detail, down to the window-fastenings; you wouldn't find another like it, in the length and breadth of England." The people to whom he said these things looked at him curiously; he spoke in a shrill, eager voice, and they thought he must be very anxious to sell. "Hard-up, no doubt," they said as they went away. Others said, "He probably belongs to a distant branch of the family, and doesn't care."

X

After the inventory men, the dealers. Cigars, paunches, check-waistcoats, signet-rings. Insolent plump hands thumbing the velvets; shiny lips pushed out in disparagement, while small eyes twinkled with concupiscence. Chase grew to know them well. Yet he taught himself to banter even with the dealers, to pretend his excessive boredom with the whole uncongenial business. He advertised his contempt for the possessions that circumstances had thrust on him; they could and should, he let it be understood, affect him solely through their marketable value. The house itself—he quoted Nutley, to the dealers not to the people who came to view—"Small rooms, dark passages, no bathrooms, no electric light." He said these things often and loudly, and laughed after he had said them as though he had uttered a witticism. The dealers laughed with him, politely, but they thought him a little wild, and from time to time cast at him a glance of slight surprise.

All this while he sent no letter to Wolverhampton.

He got one letter from his office, a typewritten letter, considerate and long-suffering, addressed to P. Chase, Esq., at the foot (he was accustomed to seeing himself referred to as "our Mr. Chase" by his firm—anyhow they hadn't ferreted out the Peregrine), suggesting that, although they quite understood that private affairs of importance were detaining him, he might perhaps for their guidance indicate an approximate date for his return. He reflected vaguely that they were treating him very decently; and dropped the letter into the wastepaper basket.

XI

H e saw, however, that he would soon have to go. He clung on, but the sale was imminent; red and black posters appeared on all the cottages; and larger, redder, and blacker posters announced the sale, "By order of Peregrine Chase, Esq.," of "the unique collection of antique furniture, tapestries, pictures, and contents of the mansion," and in types of varying size detailed these contents, so that Chase could see, flaunting upon walls, trees, and gate-posts, when he wandered out, the soulless dates and the auctioneer's bombast that advertised for others the quality of his possessions.

An illustrated booklet was likewise published. Nutley gave him a copy. "This quite unique sixteenth century residence"; "the original panelling and plasterwork"; "the moat and contemporary outbuildings"; "the old-world garden"—Chase fluttered over the pages, and rage seized him by the throat. "Nicely got up, don't you think?" Nutley said complacently.

Chase took the booklet away with him, up into the gallery. He always liked the gallery, because it was long, low, deserted, and so glowingly ornate; and more peaceful than any of the other rooms in the whole peaceful house. When he went there with the booklet in his hand that evening, he sat quite still for a time while the hush that his entrance had disturbed settled down again upon the room and its motionless occupant. A latticed rectangle of deep gold lay across the boards, the last sunlight of the day. Chase turned over the leaves of the book. "The Oak Parlour, an apartment 20 ft. by 25 ft., partially panelled in linen-fold in a state of the finest preservation," was that his library? it couldn't be, so accurate, so precise? Why, the room was living! through the windows one saw up the garden, and saw the peacocks perched on the low wall, one heard their cry as they flew up into the cedars for the night; and in the evening, in that room, the fir-cones crackled on the hearth, the dry wood kindled, and the room began to smell ever so slightly of the clean, acrid wood-smoke that never quite left it, but remained clinging even when the next day the windows were open and the warm breeze fanned into the room. He had known all that about it, although he hadn't known it was twenty foot by twenty-five. He hadn't known that the panelling against which he had been accustomed to set his bowl of coral tulips was called linen-fold.

He was an ignorant fellow; he hadn't known; he didn't know anything even now; the sooner he went back to Wolverhampton the better.

He turned over another page of the booklet. "The Great Staircase and Armorial Window, (cir. 1584) with coats-of-arms of the families of Chase, Dacre, Medlicott, and Cullinbroke,"—the window whose gaudiness always seemed to attract a peacock to parade in rivalry on the outer ledge, like the first day he had come to Blackboys; but why had they given everything such high-sounding names? the "Great Staircase," for instance; it was never called that, but only "the staircase," nor was it particularly great, only wide and polished and leisurely. He supposed Nutley was responsible, or was it Farebrother? Farebrother who was so kindly, and might have wanted to salve Chase's feelings by appealing to his vanity through the splendour of his property?

What a fool he was; of course, neither Nutley nor Farebrother gave a thought to his feelings, but only to the expediency of selling the house.

He turned the pages further. "The Long Gallery,"—here, at least, they had not tried to improve upon the usual name—"a spacious apartment running the whole length of the upper floor, 100 ft. by 30 ft. wide, sumptuously ornamented in the Italian style of the sixteenth century, with mullioned heraldic windows, overmantel of sculptured marble, rich plastered ceiling," here he raised his eyes and let them stray down the length of the gallery; the rectangle of sunlight had grown deeper and more luminous; the blocks of shadow in the corners had spread, the velvet chairs against the tapestry had merged and become yet more fruity; they were like split figs, like plums, like ripe mulberries; the colour of the room was as luxuriant as the spilling out of a cornucopia.

Chase became aware that Fortune was standing beside him.

"Mr. Nutley asked me to tell you, sir, that he couldn't wait any longer, but that he'll be here again tomorrow."

Chase blushed and stammered, as he always did when someone took him by surprise, and as he more particularly did when that someone happened to be one of his own servants. Then he saw tears standing in the old butler's eyes. He thought angrily to himself that the man was as soft-hearted as an old woman.

"Seen this little book, Fortune?" he inquired, holding it out towards him.

"Oh, sir!" exclaimed the butler, turning aside.

"Well, what's the matter? what's the matter?" said Chase, in his most irritable tone.

He got up and moved away. He went out into the garden, troubled and disquieted by the excessive tumult in his soul. He gazed down upon the mellow roofs and chimneys, veiled in a haze of blue smoke; upon all the beauty that had given him peace and content; but far from deriving comfort now he felt himself provoked by a fresh anguish, impotent and yet rebellious, a weak fury, an irresolute insubordination. Schemes, that his practical sense told him were fantastically futile, kept dashing across his mind. He would tell Fortune to shut the door in everybody's face, more especially Nutley's. He would destroy the bridge across the moat. He would sulk inside his house, admitting no one; he and his house, alone, allied against rapacity. Fortune and the few other servants might desert him if they chose; he would cook for himself, he would dust, he would think it an honour to dust; and suddenly the contrast between the picture of himself with a duster in his hand, and of himself striking at the bridge with a pickaxe, caused him to laugh out loud, a laugh bitter and tormented, that could never have issued from his throat in the Wolverhampton days. He wished that he were back in those days, again the conscientious drudge, earning enough to keep himself in decent lodgings (not among brocades and fringes, or plumed and canopied beds! not in the midst of this midsummer loveliness, that laid hands more gentle and more detaining than the hands of any woman about his heart! not this old dignity that touched his pride!), and he stared down upon the roofs of the house lying cupped in its hollow, resentful of the vision that had thus opened out as though by treachery at a turning of his drab existence, yet unable to sustain a truly resentful or angry thought, by reason of the tenderness that melted him, and the mute plea of his inheritance, that, scorning any device more theatrical, quietly relied upon its simple beauty as its only mediator.

XII

M r. Nutley was considerably relieved when he heard that Chase had gone back to Wolverhampton. From being negligible, Chase had lately become a slightly inconvenient presence at Blackboys; not that he ever criticized or interfered with the arrangements that Nutley made, but Nutley felt vaguely that he watched everything and registered internal comments; yes, although not a very sensitive chap, perhaps—he hadn't time for that—Nutley had become aware that very little eluded Chase's observation. It was odd, and rather annoying, that in spite of his taciturnity and his shy manner, Chase should so contrive to make himself felt. Any of the people on the estate, who had spoken with him more than once or twice, had a liking and a respect for him. Perhaps, Nutley consoled himself, it was thanks to tradition quite as much as to Chase's personality, and he permitted himself a little outburst against the tradition he hated, envied, and scorned.

Now that Chase had gone back to Wolverhampton, Nutley arrived more aggressively at Blackboys, rang the bell louder, made more demands on Fortune, and bustled everybody about the place.

The first time he came there in the owner's absence the dog met him in the hall, stretching himself as though just awakened from sleep, coming forward with his nails clicking on the boards.

"He misses his master," said Fortune compassionately.

Nutley thought, with discomfort, that the whole place missed Chase. There were traces of him everywhere—the obverse of his handwriting on the pad of blotting-paper in the library, his stick in the hall, and some of his clothes in a pile on the bed in his bedroom.

"Yes, Mr. Chase left a good many of his things behind," said Fortune when consulted.

"When does he think he's coming back?—the sale takes place next week," grumbled Nutley.

It was nearly midsummer; the heat-haze wickered above the ground, and the garden was tumultuous with butterflies and flowers.

"It seems a pity to think of Mr. Chase missing all this fine weather," Fortune remarked.

Nutley had no affection whatever for Fortune; he possessed the knack of making remarks to which he could not reasonably take exception, but which contrived slightly to irritate him.

"I daresay he's getting the fine weather where he is," he replied curtly.

"Ah, but in towns it isn't the same thing; when he's got his own garden here, and all," said Fortune, not yielding to Nutley, who merely shrugged, and started talking about the sale in a sharp voice.

He was in his element, Chase once dismissed from his mind. He came up to Blackboys nearly everyday, quite unnecessarily, giving every detail his attention, fawning upon anyone who seemed a likely purchaser for the house, gossiping with the dealers who now came in large numbers, and accepting their cigars with a "Well, I don't mind if I do—bit of a strain, you know, all this—the responsibility, and so on." He had the acquisitiveness of a magpie, for scraps of sale-room gossip. Dealers ticking off items in their catalogues, men in green baize aprons shifting furniture, the front door standing permanently open to all comers, were all a source of real gratification to him; while in the number of motors that waited under the shade of the trees he took a personal pride. He rubbed his hands with pleasure over the coming and going, and at the crunch of fresh wheels on the gravel. Chase's ridiculous little padlock on the wooden gate—there wasn't much trace of that now! Front door and back door were open, the summer breeze wandering gently between them and winnowing the shreds of straw that trailed about the hall, and in the passage beyond; and anyone who had finished inspecting the house might pass into the garden by the back door, to stroll up the central walk, till Nutley, looking out of an upper floor window, taking upon himself the whole credit, and full of a complacent satisfaction, thought that the place had the appearance of a garden party.

A country sale! It was one that would set two counties talking, one that would attract all the biggest swells from London (Wertheimer, Durlacher, Duveen, Partridge, they had all been already, taking notes), such a collection didn't often come under the hammer—no, by jove, it didn't! and Nutley, reading for the fiftieth time the name "Nutley, Farebrother and Co., Estate Agents and Solicitors," at the foot of the poster, reflected how that name would gain in fame and lustre by the association. Not that Farebrother, not that Co., had been allowed many fingers in the pie; he, Nutley, had done it all; it was *his* show, *his* ewe-lamb; he would have snapped the head off anyone who had dared to claim a share, or scorned them with a single glance.

He wondered to whom the house itself would ultimately fall. He had received several offers for it, but none of them had reached the reserve figure of thirty thousand. The dealers, of course, would make a ring for the furniture, the tapestries, and the pictures, and would doubtless resell them to its new owner of the house at an outrageous profit. Nutley had his eye on a Brazilian as a very probable purchaser; not only had he called at the estate office himself for all possible particulars, but on a second occasion he had brought his son and his daughter with him, exotic birds brilliantly descending upon the country solicitor's office. They had come in a white Rolls-Royce, which had immediately compelled Nutley's disapproving respect; it had a negro chauffeur on the box, the silver statuette of a nymph with streaming hair on the bonnet, and a spray of orchids in a silver and crystal vase inside. The Brazilian himself was an unpretentious cattle magnate, with a quick, clipped manner, and a wrinkled face the colour of a coffee-bean; he might be the purveyor of dollars, but he wasn't the showy one; the ostentation of the family had passed into the children. These were in their early twenties, spoilt and fretful; the tyrants of their widowed father, who listened to all their remarks with an indulgent smile. Nutley, who had never in the whole of his life seen anything like them, tried to make himself believe that he couldn't decide which was the more offensive, but, secretly, he was much impressed. "Plenty of bounce, anyway," he reflected, observing the son, his pearl-grey suit over admirably waisted stays, his black hair swept back from his brow, and shining like the flanks of a wet seal, his lean hands weighted with fat platinum rings, his walk that slightly swayed, as though the syncopated rhythm of the plantations had passed forever into his blood; and, observing him, the strangest shadow of envy passed across the shabby little solicitor in the presence of such lackadaisical youth. . . The daughter, more languid and more subtly insolent, so plump that she seemed everywhere cushioned: her tiny hands had no knuckles, but only dimples, and everything about her was round, from the single pearls on her fingers to the toecaps of her patent leather shoes. Clearly the father had offered Blackboys to the pair as an additional toy. They were as taken with it as their deliberately unenthusiastic manner would permit them to betray; and Nutley guessed that sufficient sulks on the part of the daughter would quickly induce the widower to increase his offer of twenty-five thousand by the necessary five. Up to the present he had held firm, a business convention which Nutley was ready tacitly to accept. He had reported the visit to Chase, but Chase (the unaccountable) hadn't taken much interest. Since then he had seen the brother and sister several times wandering over the house and garden, and this he took to be a promising sign. The father he hadn't seen again, but that didn't distress him: the insolent pair were the ones who counted.

XIII

Only two days remained. Chase had sent for his clothes, and had enclosed a note for Nutley in his letter to Fortune: "Press of business" prevented him from returning to Blackboys, but he was content to leave everything in Nutley's hands, etc. Polite enough. Nutley read the note, standing in the gallery which had been cleared in preparation for the sale. (It was, he thought, a stroke of genius to hold the sale in the house itself—to display the furniture in its own surroundings, instead of in the dreary frame of an auction room. That would make very little difference to the dealers, of course, who knew the intrinsic value; but from the stray buyers, the amateurs who would be after the less important things, it might mean anything up to an extra 25 percent.). He was alone in the gallery, for it was not yet ten o'clock, and he maliciously wondered what Chase's feelings would be if he could see the room now, the baize-covered tables on trestle legs, the auctioneer's desk and high chair, the rows of cane chairs arranged as though in a theatre, the choicest pieces of furniture grouped behind cords at the further end of the room, like animals awaiting slaughter in a pen. The little solicitor was from time to time startled by the stab of malice that thought of Chase evoked; he was startled now. He clapped his hand over his mouth—to suppress an exclamation, or a grin?—and glanced round the gallery. It was empty but for the lean dog, who sat with his tail curled like a whip-lash round his haunches, and who might have come down out of the tapestry, gravely regarding Nutley. The lean dog, scenting disruption, had trailed about the house for days like a haunted soul, and Nutley had fallen into the habit of saying to him, with a jocularity oddly peppered by venom, "I'll put you into the sale as an extra item, spindle-shanks."

Dimly, it gratified him to insult Chase through Chase's dog.

People began to filter in. They wandered about, looking at things and consulting their catalogues; Nutley, who examined them stealthily and with as much self-consciousness as if he had been the owner, discriminated nicely between the *bona fide* buyers and those who came out of idle curiosity. (Chase had already recognized the mentality that seizes upon any pretext for penetrating into another man's house; if as far as his bedroom, so much the better.) Nutley might as well have returned to his office since here there was no longer anything for him to do, but he lingered, with the satisfaction of an impresario. Could he but have stood at the front door, to receive the people as the cars rolled up at intervals! Hospitable and welcoming phrases came springing to his lips, and his hands spread themselves urbanely, the palms outwards. No sharpness in his manner! none of the chilblained acerbity that kept him always on the defensive! nothing but honey and suavity! "Walk in, walk in, ladies and gentlemen! No entrance fee in *my* peep show. Twenty years I had to wait for the old woman to die; I fixed my eye on her when she was sixty, but she clung on till she was over eighty; then she went. It's all in my hands now. Walk in, walk in, ladies and gentlemen; walk upstairs; the show's going to begin."

It was very warm. Really an exceptional summer. If the weather held for another two days, it would improve the attendance at the sale. London people would come (Nutley had the sudden idea of running a special). Even now, picnic parties were dotted about, under the trees beside their motors. No wonder that they were glad to exchange burning pavements against fresh grass for a day. Chase—Chase wouldn't like the litter they left. Bits of paper, bottles and tins. He wouldn't say anything; he never did; that was exactly what made him so disconcerting; but he would look, and his nose would curl. But Chase was safely away, while the picnics took place under his trees, and women in their light summer dresses strolled about in his garden and pointed with their parasols at his house. Nutley saw them from the windows. For the first time since he remembered the place, the parapet of the central walk was bare of peacocks; they had taken refuge indignantly in the cedars, where they could be heard screeching. He remembered Chase, feeding them with bits of bread from his pocket. He remembered old Miss Chase, wagging her finger at him, and saying "Ah, Nutley" (she had always called him by her surname, like a man), "you want to deprive an old maid of her children; it's too bad of you!"

But the Chases were gone, both of them, and no Chases remained, but those who stared sadly from their frames, where they stood propped against the wall ready to be carried into the sale room.

XIV

June the twenty-first. The day of the sale. Midsummer day. Nutley's day. He arrived early at the house, and met at the door Colonel Stanforth, who had walked across the park, and who considered the solicitor's umbrella with amusement. "Afraid it will rain, Nutley? Look at that blue sky, not a cloud, not even a white one." They entered the house together, Stanforth rubicund and large, Nutley noticeably spare in the black coat that enveloped him like a sheath. "Might be an undertaker's mute," Stanforth commented inwardly. "Isn't Farebrother coming up today?" he asked aloud. "Oh, yes, I daresay he'll look in later," Nutley answered, implying as clearly as possible by his tone that it was not of the slightest importance whether his partner looked in or not.

"Well, there aren't many people about yet," said Stanforth, rubbing his hands vigorously together. "What about your Brazilians, eh? Are they going to put in an appearance? Chase, I hear, is still in Wolverhampton."

"Yes," answered Nutley, "we shan't see much of *him*."

"Of course, there was no necessity for him to come, but it's odd of him to take so little interest, don't you think? Odd, I mean, as he seemed to like staying in the place, and to have got on so remarkably well with all the people around. Not that I saw anything of him when he was here. An unneighbourly sort of fellow, I should think. But to hear some of the people talk about him, by Gad, I was quite sorry he couldn't settle down here as squire."

"As you say, there was no necessity for him to come to the sale," said Nutley, frigidly ignoring the remainder of Stanforth's remarks.

"No, but if I'd been he, I don't think I could have kept away, all the same."

Nutley went off, saying he had things to see to. On the landing he met the butler with Thane slouching disconsolately after him.

"You'll see that that dog's shut up, Fortune," he snapped at him.

An air of suspense hung over everything. The sale was announced to begin at midday, because the London train arrived shortly after eleven, but before then the local attendance poured in, and many people drove up who had not previously been seen at the house, their business being with the lands or the farms: farmers in their gigs, tip-toeing awkwardly and apologetically on the polished boards of the hall while their horses were led away into the stable-yard, and there were many of the gentry too, who came in waggonettes or pony-traps. Nutley, watching and prying everywhere, observed the arrival of the latter with mixed feelings. On the one hand their presence increased the crush, but on the other hand he did not for a moment suppose they had come to buy. They came in families, shy and inclined to giggle and to herd together, squire and lady dressed almost similarly in tweed, and not differing much as to figure either, the sons very tall and slim, and slightly ashamed, the daughters rather taller and slimmer, in light muslins and large hats, all whispering together, half propitiatory, half on the defensive, and casting suspicious glances at everyone else. Amongst these groups Nutley discerned the young Brazilian, graceful as an antelope amongst cattle, and, going to the window, he saw the white Rolls-Royce silently manœuvring amongst the gigs and the waggonettes.

"Regular bean-feast, ain't it?" said Stanforth's voice behind him. "You ought to have had a merry-go-round and a gipsy booth, Nutley."

Nutley uncovered his teeth in a nervously polite smile. He looked at his watch, and decided that it was time the London motors began to arrive. Also the train was due. Most of those who came by train would have to walk from the station; it wasn't far across the village and down the avenue to the house. He could see the advance guard already, walking in batches of two and three. And there was Farebrother; silly old Farebrother, with his rosy face, and his big spectacles, and his woolly white curls under the broad hat. Not long to wait now. The auctioneer's men were at their posts; most of the chairs in the gallery were occupied, only the front rows being left empty owing to diffidence; the auctioneer himself, Mr. Webb, had arrived and stood talking to Colonel Stanforth, with an air of unconcern, on any topic other than the sale.

The farms and outlying portions were to be dealt with first, then the house and the contents of the house, then the park, and the building lots that had been carved out of the park and that were especially dear to Nutley. It would be a long sale, and probably an exciting one. He hoped there would be competition over the house. He knew that several agencies were after it, but thought that he would place his money on the Brazilian.

A continuous stir of movement and conversation filled the gallery. People came up to Nutley and asked him questions in whispers, and some of the big dealers nodded to him. Nearly all the men had their catalogues and pencils ready; some were reading the booklet. The Brazilian slipped into a prominent seat, accompanied by his solicitor.

A quarter to twelve. The garden was deserted now, for everyone had crowded into the house. Five minutes to twelve. Mr. Webb climbed up into his high chair, adjusted his glasses, and began turning over some papers on the desk before him.

A message was brought to Nutley: Mr. Webb would be much obliged if he would remain at hand to answer any point that might be raised. Nutley was only too glad. He went and leant against the auctioneer's chair, at the back, and from there surveyed the whole length of the room. Rows of expectant people. People leaning against the walls and in the doorways. The gaitered farmers. The gentry. The dealers. The clerks and small fry. The men in green baize aprons. Such a crowd as the gallery had never seen.

"Lot 1, gentlemen. . ."

The sharp rap of the auctioneer's little ivory hammer, and the buzz in the room was stilled; throats were cleared, heads raised.

"Lot 1, gentlemen. Three cottages adjoining the station, with one acre of ground; coloured green on plan. What bids, gentlemen? Anyone start the bidding? Five hundred guineas? four hundred? Come, come, gentlemen, please," admonishing them, "we have a great deal to get through. I ask your kind co-operation."

Knocked down at seven hundred and fifty guineas. Nutley noted the sum in the margin of his catalogue. Webb was a capital auctioneer: he bustled folk, he chaffed them, he got them into a good temper, he made them laugh so that their purses laughed wide in company. He had a jolly round face, a twinkling eye, and a rose-bud in his buttonhole. Five hundred and fifty for the next lot, two cottages; so far, so good.

"Now, gentlemen, we come to something a little more interesting: the farm-house and lands known as Orchards. An excellent house, and a particularly fine brew of ale kept there, too, as I happen to know—though that doesn't go with the house." (The audience laughed; it appreciated that kind of pleasantry.) "What offers, gentlemen? Two hundred acres of fine pasture and arable, ten acres of shaw, twenty acres of first-class fruit-trees. . ." "That's so, sir," from Chase's old apple-dealer friend at the back of the room, and heads were turned smilingly towards him. "There spoke the best authority in the county," cried the auctioneer, catching on to this, "as nice a little property as you could wish. I've a good mind to start the bidding myself. Fifty guineas—I'll put up fifty guineas. Who'll go one better?" The audience laughed again; Mr. Webb had a great reputation as a wag. Nutley caught sight of Farebrother's full-moon face at the back of the room, perfunctorily smiling.

The tenant began bidding for his own farm; he had been to Nutley to see whether a mortgage could be arranged, and Nutley knew the extent of his finances. The voice of the auctioneer followed the bidding monotonously up, "Two thousand guineas. . . two thousand two hundred. . . come, gentlemen, we're wasting time. . . two thousand five hundred. . ."

Knocked down to the farmer at three thousand five hundred guineas. A wink passed between Nutley and the purchaser: the place had not sold very well, but Nutley's firm would get the commission on the mortgage.

Lot 4. Jakes' cottage. Nutley remembered that Chase had once commented on Jakes' garden, and he remembered also that old Miss Chase used to favour Jakes and his flowers; he supposed sarcastically that it was hereditary among the Chases to favour Jakes. That same stab of malice came back to him, and this time it included Jakes: the man made himself ridiculous over his garden, carrying (as he boasted) soil and leaf-mould home for it for miles upon his back; that was all over now, and his cottage would first be sold as a building site and then pulled down.

He caught sight of Jakes, standing near a window, his everyday corduroy trousers tied as usual with string round the knees; he looked terribly embarrassed, and was swallowing hard; the Adam's apple in his throat moved visibly above his collar. He stood twisting his cap between his hands. Nutley derisively watched him, saying to himself that the fellow might be on the point of making a speech. Surely he wasn't going to bid! a working-man on perhaps forty shillings a week! Nutley was taken up and entertained by this idea, when a stir at the door distracted his attention; he glanced to see who the late-comer was, and perceived Chase.

XV

C hase entered hurriedly, and asked a question of a man standing by; he looked haggard and ill, but the answer to his question appeared to reassure him, and he slipped quietly to the chair that somebody offered him. Several people recognized him, and pointed him out to one another. Nutley stared, incredulous and indignant. Just like his sly ways again! Why take the trouble to write and say he was detained by press of business, when he had every intention of coming? Sly. Well, might he enjoy himself, listening to the sale of his house; Nutley, with an angry shrug, wished him joy.

Meanwhile Mr. Webb's voice, above him, continued to advocate Jakes' cottage, "either as a building site or as a tea-room, gentlemen; I needn't point out to you the advantages of either in the heart of a picturesque village on a well-frequented motor route. The garden's only a quarter of an acre, but you have seen it today on your way from the station; a perfect picture. What offers? Come! We're disposed to let this lot go cheap as the cottage is in need of repair. It's a real chance for somebody."

"One hundred guineas," called out a fat man, known to Nutley as the proprietor of an hotel in Eastbourne.

"And fifty," said Jakes in a trembling voice.

Nutley suppressed a cackle of laughter.

"And seventy-five," said the fat man, after glaring at Jakes.

"Two hundred," said Jakes.

Chase sat on the edge of his chair, twisting his fingers together and keeping his eyes fixed on Jakes. So the man was trying to save his garden!—and the flowers, through whose roots he said he would put a bagginhook sooner than let them pass to a stranger. Where did he imagine he could get the money? poor fool. The fat man was after the cottage for some commercial enterprise. What had the auctioneer suggested?—a tea-room? That was it, without a doubt—a tea-room! A painted sign-board hanging out to attract motorists; little tin tables in the garden, perhaps, on summer evenings.

The fat man ran Jakes up to two hundred and fifty before Jakes began to falter. Something in the near region of two hundred and fifty was the limit, Chase guessed, to which his secret and inscrutable financial preparations would run. What plans had he made before coming, poor chap; what plans, full of a lamentable pathos, to meet the rivalry of those who might possibly have designs upon his tenement? Surely not very crafty plans, or very adequate? They had reached two hundred and seventy-five. Jakes was distressed; and to Nutley, scornfully watching, as to Chase, compassionately watching, and as to the auctioneer, impartially watching, it was clear that neither conscience nor prudence counselled him to go any further.

"Two hundred and seventy-five guineas are bid," said the voice of the auctioneer; "two hundred and seventy-five guineas,"—pause—"going, going. . ."

"Three hundred," brought out Jakes, upon whose forehead sweat was standing.

"And ten," said the fat man remorselessly.

Jakes shook his head as the auctioneer looked at him in inquiry.

"Three hundred and ten guineas *are* bid," said the auctioneer, "three hundred and ten guineas," his voice rising and trailing, "no more?—a little more, sir, come!" in persuasion to Jakes, who shook his head again. "Lot 4, gentlemen, going for the sum of three hundred and ten guineas, going, going, gone." The hammer came down with a sharp tap, and Mr. Webb leant across his desk to take the name and address of the purchaser.

Jakes began making his way out of the room. He had the shameful air of one who has failed before all men in the single audacity of his lifetime. For him, Lot 4 had been the lot that must rivet everyone's attention; it had been not an episode but the apex. Chase saw him slink out, burdened by disgrace. It would be several hours before he regained the spirit to put the bagginhook through the flowers.

"Lot 5. . ." Callous as Roman sports proceeding on the retreat of the conquered gladiator. Scatter sand on the blood! Chase sat on, dumbly listening, the auctioneer's voice and the rap of the hammer twanging, metallic, across the chords of his bursting head. He had surely been mad to come,—to expose himself to this pain, madder than poor Jakes, who at least came with a certain hope. What had brought him—his body felt curiously light; he knew only that he had slipped out of his lodgings at six that morning, had found his way into trains, his limbs performing the necessary actions for him, while his mind continued remote and fixed only upon the distant object towards which he was being rapidly carried. His house—during this miserable week in Wolverhampton, what had they been doing to his house?—

perpetrating what infamy? Sitting in the train his mind glazed into that one concentration—Blackboys; he had wondered dimly whether he would indeed find the place where he had left it, among the trees, or whether he had dreamt it, under an enchantment; whether life in Wolverhampton—his office, his ledgers, his clerks, his lodgings—were not the only reality? Still his limbs, intelligent servants, had carried him over the difficulties of the cross-country journey, rendering him at the familiar station—a miracle. As he crossed the stile at the bend of the footpath—for he had taken the short cut across the fields from the station—he had come upon the house, he had heard his breath sob in his throat, and he had repressed the impulse to stretch out both his hands. . . With his eagerness his steps had quickened. It was the house, though not as he knew it. Not slumbrous. Not secluded. Carriages and motors under the trees, grooms and chauffeurs strolling about, idly staring. The house unveiled, prostituted; yes, it was like seeing one's mistress in a slave-market. He had bounded up the steps into the hall, where a handful of loafing men had quizzed him impertinently. The garden door opposite, stood open, and he could see right up the garden; was puzzled, in passing, because he missed the peacocks parading the blazon of their spread tails. The familiarity of the proportions closed instantly round him. Wolverhampton receded; *this* was reality; *this* was home.

He had gone up the staircase, his head reeling with anger when he saw that the pictures had been taken down from their places, and stood propped along the walls of the upper passage, ticketed and numbered. He had madly resented this interference with his property. Then he had gone into the gallery, sick and blind, dazzled by the sight that met him there, as though he had come suddenly into too strong a light. He had assured himself at once that they had not yet reached the selling of the house. Still his—and he stumbled into a chair and assisted at the demolition of Jakes.

The windows were wide open; bees blundered in and out; the tops of the woods appeared, huge green pillows; above them the cloudless sky; Midsummer day. Where, then, was the sweet harmony of the house and garden that waited upon the lazy hours of such a day?—driven out by dust and strangers, the Long Gallery made dingy by rows of chairs, robbed of its own mellow furnishing, robbed of its silence by sharp voices; the violation of sanctuary. Chase sat with his fingers knotted together between his knees. Perhaps a score of people in that room knew him by sight; to the others he was an onlooker; to the ones who knew him, an owner hoping for a good price. They must know he was poor—the park fence was lichen-covered and broken down in many places; the road up to the house was overgrown with weeds. Poor— obliged to sell; the place, for all its beauty, betrayed its poverty. Only the farmers looked prosperous. (Those farmers must have prospered better than they ever admitted, for here was one of them buying-in at a most respectable figure the house and lands he rented.) His over-excited senses quietening down a little, he paid attention to the progress of the sale, finding there nothing but the same intolerable pain; the warmth of his secret memory stirred by the chill probe of the words he heard pronounced from the auctioneer's desk—"ten acres of fallow, known as Ten-Acre Field, with five acres, three roods, and two perches of wood, including a quantity of fine standing timber to the value of two hundred and fifty pounds"—he knew that wood; it was free of undergrowth, and the bare tree-trunks rose like columns straight out of a sea of bluebells: two hundred and fifty pounds' worth of standing timber. Walking in Ten-Acre Field outside the edge of that wood he had scared many a rabbit that vanished into the wood with a frisk of white tail, and had startled the rusty pheasants up into heavy flight.

Knocked down to the farmer who had just bought in his farm.

He didn't much resent the fields and woods going to the farmers. If anyone other than himself must have them, let it be the yeomen by whom they were worked and understood. But the house—there was the rub, the anguish. Nutley had mentioned a Brazilian (Nutley's most casual word about the house, or a buyer for the house, had remained indelibly stamped on Chase's mind). He looked about now, for the first time since he had come into the room, and discovered Nutley leaning against the auctioneer's high chair, then he discovered the young man who must certainly be the Brazilian in question, and all the dread which had been hitherto, so to speak, staved off, now smote him with its imminence as his eyes lighted on the unfamiliar, insouciant face.

The new owner, lounging there, insufferable, graceful, waiting without impatience, so insultingly unperturbed! Cool as a cucumber, that young man, accustomed to find life full of a persevering amiability. Chase made a movement to rise; he wanted to fly the room, to escape an ordeal that appalled his soul, but his shyness held him down: he could not create a sensation before so many people. Enraged as he was by the absurd weakness that caught him thus, and prevented him from saving himself while there was still time, he yet submitted, pinned to his chair, enduring such misery as made all his previous grief sink to the level of mere discomfort. He yearned even after hours that lay in the past, and that at the time of their being had seemed to him, in all truth, sufficiently weighted; the hours he had spent standing beside the dealers during their minute examination of his possessions, while he wrung out his pitiable flippancies; then, in those days, he had known that ultimately they would take their leave, and that he would be left to turn back alone into his house, greeted by the dog beating his tail against the legs of the furniture, as pleased as his master; or the hour when, sitting in this very gallery (how different then!), he had read through Nutley's offensive booklet, and had not known whether it was chiefly anger or pain that drove extravagant ideas of revolt across his mind; those hours by comparison now appeared to him elysian—he had tasted then but the froth on the cup of bitterness of which he now reached the dregs.

God! how quickly they were getting through the lots! Lot 14 was already reached, and 16 was the house. Surely no soul could withstand such pressure, but must crumble like a crushed shell? When they actually reached Lot 16, when he heard the auctioneer start off with his "Now, gentlemen. . ." what would he do then? how would he behave? It was no longer shyness that held him, but fascination, and a physical sickness that made his body clammy and moist although he was shivering with cold. Fear must be like this, and from his heart he pitied all those who were mortally afraid. He noticed that several people were looking at him, amongst others Nutley, and he thought that he must be losing control of his reason, for it seemed to him that Nutley's face was yellow and pointed, and was grinning at him with a squinting malevolence, an oblique derision, altogether fantastic, and pushed up quite close to him, although in reality Nutley was some way off. He put up his hand to his forehead, and one or two people made an anxious movement towards him, as though they thought he was going to faint. He rejected them with a vague gesture, and at that moment heard the auctioneer say, "Lot 16, gentlemen. . ."

XVI

There was a general stir in the room, of chairs being shifted, and legs uncrossed and recrossed. Mr. Webb gave a little cough, while he laid aside his catalogue in favour of the more elaborate booklet, which he opened on the desk in front of him, flattening down the pages with a precise hand. He drew himself up, took off his glasses, and tapped the booklet with them, surveying his audience. "As you know, ladies and gentlemen—as, in fact, this monograph, which you have all had in your hands, will have told you if you did not know it before—we have in Blackboys one of the most perfect examples of the Elizabethan manor-house in England. I don't think I need take up your time and my own by enlarging upon that, or by pointing out the historical and artistic value of the property about to be disposed of; I can safely leave the ancient building, and the monograph so ably prepared by my friend Mr. Nutley, to speak for themselves. It only remains for me to beg those intending to bid, to second my efforts in putting the sale through as quickly as possible, for we still have a large portion of the catalogue to deal with, and to bear in mind that a reserve figure of reasonable proportions has been placed upon the manor-house and surrounding grounds.—Lot 16, the manor-house known as Blackboys Priory, the pleasure-grounds of eight acres, and one hundred and twenty-five acres of park land adjoining."

A short silence succeeded Mr. Webb's little speech. The Brazilian and his solicitor whispered together. The representatives of the various agencies looked at one another to see who would take the first step. Finally a voice said, "Eight thousand guineas."

"Come, come," smiled Mr. Webb.

"Nine thousand," said another voice.

"I told you, gentlemen, that a reasonable reserve had been placed upon this lot," said the auctioneer in a tone of restrained impatience, "and you must all of you be sufficiently acquainted with the standard of sale-room prices to know that nine thousand guineas comes nowhere near a reasonable figure for a property such as the one we have now under consideration."

Thus rebuked, the man who had first spoken said, "All right—twelve thousand."

"And five hundred," said the second man.

"Sticky, sticky," murmured Nutley, shaking his head.

Still neither the Brazilian nor his solicitor made any sign. The agents were evidently unwilling to show their hands; then a little man began to bid on behalf of an American standing at his elbow: "Thirteen thousand guineas."

This stirred the agents, and between them all the bidding crackled up to eighteen thousand. Mr. Webb, judging that the American was probably good for twenty or twenty-five, and wishing to entice the Brazilian into competition, said in the same resigned tone, "I am unwilling to withdraw this lot, but I am afraid we cannot afford to waste time in this fashion."

"Make it twenty, sir," called out the American, "and let's get a move on."

"Thank you, sir," said Mr. Webb, in the midst of a laugh. "I am bid twenty thousand guineas for Lot 16, twenty thousand guineas *are* bid. . . and five hundred on my right. . . twenty-one thousand on my left. . . thank you again, sir: twenty-two thousand guineas. Twenty-two thousand guineas. Surely no one wishes to see this lot withdrawn? Twenty-two thousand guineas. And five hundred. And two hundred and fifty more. Twenty-two thousand seven hundred and fifty guineas. . ."

"Twenty-three thousand," said the solicitor who had come with the Brazilian.

People craned forward now to see and to hear. The Brazilian had been generally pointed out as the most likely buyer, and until he or his man took up the bidding it could be disregarded as preliminary. The small fry of the agents served to run it up into workable figures, after which it would certainly pass beyond them. The duel, it was guessed, would lie between the American and the Brazilian.

"Twenty-four thousand," called out one of the agents in a sort of dying flourish.

"And five hundred," said another, not to be outdone.

"Twenty-five thousand," said the Brazilian's solicitor.

"Twenty-five thousand guineas *are* bid," said the auctioneer. "Twenty-five thousand guineas. I am authorised by Mr. Nutley, the solicitor acting for this estate, to tell you. . ." he glanced down at Nutley, who nodded, ". . . to tell you that this sum had already been offered, and refused, at the estate office. If, therefore, no gentleman is willing to pass beyond twenty-five thousand guineas, I shall be compelled. . . and five hundred, thank you, sir. Twenty-five thousand five hundred guineas."

Most people present supposed that this sum came very near to being adequate, and a murmur to this effect passed up and down the room. People looked at Chase, who was as white as death and sat with his eye fixed upon the floor. The American, good-humouredly enough, was trying to take the measure of the unruffled young man; judging from the slight shrug he gave, he did not think he stood much chance, but nevertheless he called, "Keep the ball rolling. Two hundred and fifty more."

The room began to take sides, most preferring the straight forward vulgarity of the jolly American to the outlandishness of the young man, which baffled and put them ill at their ease. (Nutley found time to think that the youth of the neighbourhood would need sometime before it recovered from the influence of that young man, even if he were to pass away with the day.) Those who had the habit of sale-rooms thought Chase lucky in having two men, both keen, against one another to run up a high price. They bent forward with their elbows on their knees and their chins in their hands, to listen.

"And two hundred and fifty more," capped the solicitor.

"Twenty-six thousand guineas are bid," said Mr. Webb, who by now was leaning well over his desk and whose glances kept travelling sharply between the rivals. He was sure that the Brazilian intended, if necessary, to go to thirty thousand.

"Twenty-seven," said the American, recklessly.

"Twenty-eight," said the solicitor after a word with his employer.

The American shook his head; he was very jovial and friendly, and bore no malice. He laughed, but he shook his head.

"If that is your last word, gentlemen, I regret to say that the lot must be withdrawn, as the reserve has not been reached," said Mr. Webb. "I am sure that Mr. Nutley will pardon me the slight irregularity in giving you this information, under the exceptional circumstances. . ." Nutley assented; he greatly enjoyed being referred to, especially now in Chase's presence. . . "I only do so in order to give you the chance of continuing should you wish. . ."

"All right, anything to make a running," said the American, who was certainly the favourite of the excited and eager audience; "two hundred and fifty better than the last bid."

The auctioneer caught the Brazilian's nod.

"I am bid twenty-eight thousand five hundred guineas. . . twenty-nine thousand," he added, as the American nodded to him.

"Thirty," said the Brazilian quietly.

He had not spoken before, and every gaze was turned upon him as, perfectly cool, he stood leaning against the wall in the bay of a window. He was undisturbed, from the sleekness of his head down to his immaculate shoes. He had all the assurance of one who is certain of having spoken the last word.

"I'm out of this," said the American.

"Thirty thousand guineas *are* bid," said the auctioneer; "for Lot 16 thirty thousand guineas. THIRTY THOUSAND GUINEAS," he enunciated; "going, for the sum of thirty thousand guineas, going, going. . ."

Chase tottered to his feet.

"Thirty-one thousand," he cried in a strangled voice, "thirty-one thousand!"

XVII

O f all the astonished people in that room, perhaps not the least astonished was the auctioneer. He had never seen Chase before, and naturally thought that he had to deal with an entirely new candidate. He adjusted his glasses to stare at the solitary figure upright among the rows of seated people, standing with a trembling hand still outstretched. He had just time to notice with concern that Chase was deathly pale, his face carved and hollowed, before habit reasserted itself, and he checked the "gone!" that had almost left his lips, to resume his chronicle of the bidding with "Thirty-one thousand guineas. . . any advance on thirty-one thousand guineas?" and cocked his eye at the Brazilian.

The Brazilian, equally surprised, had never before seen Chase either. What was this fierce little man, who had shot up out of the ground so turbulently to dispute his prize? He had not supposed that it would be necessary to go beyond the thirty thousand; nevertheless he was prepared to do so, and to make his determination clear he continued with the bidding himself instead of leaving it to his solicitor. "And five hundred," he said.

"Thirty-five thousand," said Chase.

The sensation he would have created by escaping from the room half an hour earlier was nothing to the sensation he was creating now. But he was exalted far beyond shyness or false shame. He never noticed the excited flutter all over the room, or the extraordinary agitation of Nutley, who was saying "He's mad! he's mad!" while frantically trying to attract the auctioneer's attention. Chase was oblivious to all this. He stood, feeling himself inspired by some divine breath, the room a blur before him, and a current of power, quite indomitable, surging through his veins. Infatuation. Genius. They must be like this. This certainty. This unmistakable purpose. This sudden clearing away of all irrelevant preoccupations. Vistas opened down into all the obscurities that had always shadowed and confused his brain: the secret was to find oneself, to know what one really wanted, what one really cared for, and to go for it straight. Wolverhampton? moonshine! He was no longer pale, nor did he keep his eyes shamefully bent upon the ground; he was flushed, embattled; his nostrils dilated and working.

But everyone else thought him crazy, people sober watching the vaingloriousness of a man drunk. Even the auctioneer allowed an expression of surprise to cross his face, and varied his formula by saying suavely, "Did I understand you to say thirty-five thousand, sir? Thirty-five thousand guineas are bid."

Drunk. As a man drunk. Everything appeared smothered to his senses; intense, yet remote. His head light and swimming. Everything at a great distance. The crowd around him, stirring, murmurous, but meaningless. The auctioneer, perched up there, a diminutive figure, miles away. Voices, muffled but enormously significant, conveying threats, conveying combat. All leagued against him. This was battle; all the faces were hostile. Or so he imagined. He was glad of it. Fighting for his house? no, no! more, far more than that: fighting for the thing he loved. Fighting to shield from rape the thing he loved. Fighting alone; come to his senses in the very nick of time. Even at this moment, when he needed every wit he had ever had at his command, he found time for a deep inward thankfulness that the illumination had not come too late or altogether passed him by. In the nick of time it had come, and he had recognized it; recognized it for what it was, and seized hold of it, and now, triumphantly, drunkenly, was holding his own in the face of all this dismay and opposition. Moreover, they could not defeat him. Bidding in these outrageous sums that need never be paid over, he was possessed of an inexhaustible fortune. Undefeatable—what confidence that gave him! The more hands turned against him the better. He challenged everybody; he hardly knew what he was saying, only that he leapt up in thousands, and that in spite of their astonishment and fury they were powerless against him: there was nothing criminal or even illegal in his buying-in his own house if he wanted to.

And then the end, that came before he knew that it was imminent; the collapse of the Brazilian, whose expression had at last changed from deliberate indifference to real bad temper; the voice of the auctioneer, suavely asking for his name and his address; and his own voice, giving his name as though for the first time in his life he were not ashamed of it. And then Nutley, struggling across the room to him, snarling and yapping at him like a little enraged cur, quite vague and deprived of significance, but withal noisy, tiresome, and briefly perplexing; a Nutley disproportionately enraged, furiously gesticulating, spluttering at him, "Are you going to play this damned fool game with the rest of the sale?" and his answer—he supposed he had given an answer, because of the announcement from the auctioneer's desk, which hushed the noisy room into sudden silence, "I have to inform you, gentlemen, that Lot

16, and the succeeding lots, which include the contents of the mansion, also the surrounding park, have been bought in, and that the sale is therefore at an end."

And, in the midst of his bewilderment, the sensation of having his hand sought for and wrung, while he gazed down into Mr. Farebrother's old rosy face and heard him say, half inarticulate with emotion, "I'm so glad, Mr. Chase, I congratulate you, I'm so glad, I'm so *glad*."

XVIII

Finally, the blessed peace and solitude, when the last stranger with the curious stare that was now common to them all had quitted the house, and the last motor had rolled away. Chase, leaning against a column of the porch, thought that thus must married lovers feel when after the confusion of their wedding they are at length left alone together. Certainly—with a wry twist to his lip—the events of the sale had tried him as sorely as any wedding. But here he was, having won, in possession, having driven away all that rabble; here he was in the warmth, and in the hush that sank back upon everything after the ceasing of all that hubbub; here he was left alone upon the field after that reckless victory. Poor? yes! but he could work, he would manage; his poverty would not be bitter, it would be sweet. He suddenly stretched out his hands and passionately laid them, palms flattened, against the bricks; bricks warm as their own rosiness with the sun they had drunk since morning.

Midsummer day. Swallows skimming after the insects above the moat. Their level wings almost grazed the water as they swooped. Midsummer day. All the mellowness of Blackboys, all the blood of the Chases, to culminate in this midsummer day. A marvellous summer. A persistently marvellous summer. He remembered the procession of days, the dawns and the dusks and the moon-bathed nights, that had hallowed his romance. He was inclined to believe that neither hatred nor its ugly kin could any longer find any place in his heart, which had been so uplifted and had seen so radiantly the flare of so many beacons lighting up the fields of wisdom. To cast off the slavery of the Wolverhamptons of this world. To know what one really wanted, what one really cared for, and to go for it straight. Wasn't that a good enough and simple enough working wisdom for a man to have attained? Simple enough, when it did nobody any harm—yet so few seemed to learn it.

Blackboys! Wolverhampton! what was Wolverhampton beside Blackboys? What was the promise of that mediocre ease beside the certainty of these exquisite privations? What was that drudgery beside this beauty, this pride, this Quixotism?

Thane gambolled out, fawning and leaping round Chase, as Fortune opened the door of the house.

"Will you be having dinner, sir," he asked demurely, "in the dining-room or in the garden this evening?"

THE CHRISTMAS PARTY

To A.

I

The street door opened straight into the shop. The shop went back a long way, and was very dark and crowded with objects; everything seemed to have something else super-imposed upon it, either set down or hanging; thus against the walls dangled bunches of masks, like bunches of bananas, weapons of all kinds, shields and breastplates, swags of tinsel jewellery, wigs; upon the tops of the cupboards stood ewers, goblets, candelabra, all in sham gold plate; and the counters themselves were strewn with a miscellany of smaller theatrical necessities. It was only little by little that the glance, growing accustomed to the obscurity of the shop, began to disentangle object from object in this assortment. Everything was very dusty, with the exception of the shields and stray pieces of armour, which were brightly furbished and detached themselves like mirrors in their places on the walls, giving a distorted reflection in miniature of the recesses of the shop. There were stuffed animals, particularly dusty, with glass eyes and red open mouths showing two rows of teeth. There were grotesque cardboard heads, four times life-size, for giants. There was the figure of a knight in a complete suit of armour, with a faded blue cloak embroidered with the lilies of France hanging from his shoulders, and a closed helmet from which sprang a tuft of plumes that had once been white, but that were now grey with dust and age. This knight stood on the lowest step of the staircase that started in the middle of the shop and led to the upper floors of the house. A door across the top of the flight shut off the secrets of the upper storey from the observation of customers in the shop on the ground floor.

On the upper floors the house was old and rambling. It straggled up and down on different levels, along dark passages and into irregular little rooms, badly lit by small windows, and, like the shop, encumbered with objects; not only by the furniture, which was much too bulky for the size of the rooms, but also by properties which belonged to the shop, and which at various times had been huddled upstairs in the course of a clearance below. There were rows of dresses hanging on hooks, halberts and muskets propped up in the corners, albums of photographs for reference lying on the tables, pairs of boots and buskins thrust away behind the curtains and under the valences. You felt convinced that every drawer was packed so that it could only just be induced to shut, and that if you opened the door of a cupboard a crowd of imprisoned articles would come tumbling out helter-skelter. Everything was old and fusty; tawdry, and pretentious under its grime. Outside, the snow had gathered in tiny drifts along the leadwork of the latticed windows, making the rooms darker than they already were, and had heaped itself against the panes two or three inches above the window-sills. In the mornings the frost left fern-frond patterns on the panes; but although it was thus rendered almost impossible to see out, the bright frost and snow were a not unpleasant relief, for they were something clean and fresh, something of quite recent arrival and of certain departure, in contrast to the contents of the house, which had lain there accumulating for so many years, and which offered no promise of a disturbing hand in the years to come.

II

Over the shop door, on to the street, gold letters on a black ground said: LYDIA PROTHEROE, Theatrical Costumier and Wig-maker. Lydia was not the name by which the proprietress of the shop had been baptized, neither was Protheroe the name of her parents; her husband's name it could not be for she had never had a husband. What her real name was she had long since preferred to forget, and it was not difficult to do so, for as Lydia Protheroe she had made her fame, and in the town where she had come as a stranger there was no one to know her as anything else. The fame and the business she had built up together, amorously, jealously. It had taken her forty years. Somewhere back in the eighties she saw herself, young, determined, deaf to the outcry of her family; a young woman in a bombazine gown, with smooth bands of hair like Christina Rossetti, and arms folded, each hand clasping the opposite elbow; she saw herself thus, standing up, surveying the circle of her relations as they expostulated around her. They were outraged, they were aggrieved; they were respectable people who naturally disapproved of the stage; and here was Lydia—only to them she had not been Lydia, but Alice—announcing her intention of setting up a business which would engage her inevitably in theatrical circles. That a young woman should think of setting up business on her own account was bad enough, but such a business was an affront beyond discussion. She would bring shame upon them (here the personality of Lydia Protheroe first brilliantly germinated in Alice's mind). They threw up their hands. Alice, who might enjoy all the advantages of a gentlewoman; Alice, who might reasonably have looked for a husband, a home, a family, of her own; Alice, who up to the age of twenty-one had given them scarcely any anxiety, who had been so very genteel, all things considered—in spite of a certain element of Puckishness in her which had peeped out so very rarely, a certain disrespect of their ideals—a mere trifle, a mere indication, had they but had the wit to read, of what was brewing beneath.

And what did she reply to their remonstrance? In what phrase, maddening because irrefutable, did she finally take refuge? That she was of age.

It was true. She was twenty-one, and she had a thousand pounds left her by her grandfather. She could snap her fingers at them all if she chose. She did not literally snap her fingers; she was gentle and regretful, she said she did not wish to cut herself adrift from her family, and saw no reason why they should cut themselves adrift from her. She would not bring their name into disrepute. She would trade under another name; she would cease to be Alice Jennings, she would become Lydia Protheroe. Secretly she was elated to escape from a name of whose homeliness she had always been ashamed, but this she was careful not to betray to her family; to her family she made the announcement with an air of sacrifice. Since they were humiliated by her, and by the trade she had chosen, she would go away; she would conceal her identity in a distant town. No; she shook her smooth head in answer to their protestations; what she had declared she would carry out; they should never say they had cause to blush whenever they opened a theatre programme. "Wigs by Jennings." That should not offend their eyes. "Wigs by Protheroe," and they could sit snugly in their stalls, being Jennings, looking Jennings; connected with the stage in anyway? oh dear, no! Let them only think kindly of her in her lonely and distant— yes, distant—struggles. No doubt Miss Protheroe would find it hard at first, unfriended and unsupported; but armed with her thousand pounds she would survive the first reverses; and adversity was good for the character. Indeed, as she talked, always gentle and regretful, but perfectly obdurate, she felt her character stiffening under the test of this first adversity. The Presbyterian that was in her, as it was in all her relatives, welcomed in its austere and cheerless fashion this trial that made a demand upon her endurance. She enjoyed the self-satisfaction of the martyr. And yet, secretly, all the while, a little voice gibed at her "Hypocrite!" She knew her hypocrisy because, in spite of her affectation of martyrdom, she was rejoicing in her new isolation. She knew that she would embark on her adventure with a greater gusto since she was not to embark on it with the approval of her family. It was all very well for her to appeal to their sympathy with poor Miss Protheroe, unfriended and unsupported; the phrase sounded well, but the truth was that she wanted neither their friendship nor their support. "I want to get away from all this," she cried suddenly and despairingly. She wanted independence; she wanted the fight. She would have been defrauded of both, by the lap of a comfortable middle-class family spread out behind her to receive her if she fell. Backed up by her family, she would have felt herself backed up by the whole of the English middle-class, cushioned, solid in the consciousness of its homogeneity and resources, an enormous family of Jennings, swarming in every town and with its place of assembly in every town-hall, inimical to the exotic, mistrustful of the new, tenacious of the conventions that were as cement to its masonry; a class sagacious and shrewd, nicely knowing safety from danger, and knowing, above all, its own mind, since nothing was ever admitted to that mind to which it could not immediately affix a label. This was the class to whose protection Alice Jennings had the birthright now rejected by Lydia Protheroe. She marvelled how she could have endured it for so many years. She made a gesture as she finally rejected it; the hands that had been clasping the elbows were unloosed, and the right hand tossed up in a gesture definitely histrionic, as one who tosses a feather to the wind. Her family had almost groaned when they saw it, for they recognized it as a defiance, a symbol and an enemy. She stood there, in their midst, a slim revolutionary, not visibly tremulous, and although her hair still lay in those sleek bands plastered down on her forehead, they felt that the moment was near at hand when they would cease to be sleek and would become rumpled; even curly; even puffed out; and that the snuff-coloured bombazine of her gown would become metamorphosed into some gaudy intolerable fustian. They looked at her as though they were looking their last. They uttered a preliminary caution; she smiled. Seeing her smile, they ceased the expostulations which had been wrung from them in their first dismay; they gathered themselves up in dignity and sorrow; they said that since nothing would turn her from this reckless, this unbecoming, this. . . in short, this idea, and that since she was of age, as she had not scrupled to remind them, she must, they supposed, be allowed to follow her own course. But let her not expect to return to them when the consequences of her folly were heavy upon her. Let her not (it was her father who enunciated this figure of speech, shaking his finger solemnly at her), let her not hope to exchange for the glare of the lamplight the oil-lamp of the warm parlour of home. Once an outcast she should remain an outcast forever. She had a sudden attack of panic as these impressive words boomed upon her ears. She saw herself alone in a deserted theatre, the holland covers over the stalls, the lights turned out, and the great pit of the stage yawning at her in front of the gaunt skeleton of the scenery; and simultaneously she saw the circle of her family—who were, after all, familiar, even if not particularly enlivening—seated at their snug evening tasks in the glow of that oil-lamp of which her father had reminded her. She came near to weakening; she knew that if she held out her hands to them, even now, they would receive her again into their bosom—but how they would cackle over her! they would pat her kindly; they would talk of her having come to her senses, of being once more their little Alice; and this her pride would not endure. She discovered that she could tolerate patronage even less than security; and for the rest of her days, if she capitulated now, she would be at the mercy of her family. She would be among them on sufferance. Sooner any loneliness, any quandary, sooner even starvation, than shelter on such terms. Inclining her head, she accepted her ostracism without a protest. As soon as she had accepted it—as soon, that is, as the worst had been definitely spoken and she had definitely survived it—she felt the sense of her liberty flooding over her. Her very name dropped from her like a piece of old skin. She became that unique being, the person who has no relations. Alice Jennings had had relations, Lydia Protheroe had none, Lydia Protheroe had never even had a mother. Independence could scarcely go further. She swept one last slow look around their circle, and passed out of the room.

III

After she had left them—for she had gone then and there, in her own phrase, "out into the night"—they had uttered, when they recovered a little from their consternation, all the things they might have been expected to utter. They were very hot and angry. Her father, a stout man, had blown out his cheeks, tugged at his whiskers and pronounced, "No daughter of mine." It was an excommunication. "The ingratitude. To think that ever. . ." her mother had whimpered. Her aunt, who was elderly, frail, and timorous, had bleated, "Oh, and to think of all the *horrible* men in the world." Her brother, a severely good young man, had said, "All I ask, father, and you, too, mother, is that I may NEVER hear her name again," and his wife, who was like a little brown wren, his mere echo, had said, "Oh, dear, it does seem hard, doesn't it? but Bertie is always right about these things."

Her sister, who was engaged, summed up their main unspoken thought as she said fretfully and anxiously, "But what are we to say to people?"

IV

Lydia Protheroe, whose mind worked instinctively in terms of drama, always saw herself afterwards, in retrospect, standing alone in the rain on the pavement outside her father's house wondering where she should go. She had not expected events to be so rapid or so complete. She had foreseen long weeks of argument, during which her family would slowly be worn down to some reluctant compromise, and although this had not been much to her satisfaction as a prospect, she had resigned herself to hope for nothing more. She found herself now, triumphant indeed, but a little disconcerted, with no luggage and too much pride to slip into the house again in order to pack. No doubt they counted on her doing so; no doubt their ultimatum had been but bluff. Probably they were even now sitting expectant, waiting to hear her key in the door, waiting to rush out and overwhelm her in the passage, and to pull her in with cries of "Alice, dear, we didn't mean it!" Let them wait! She started down the wet street, where the gas-lamps shone reflected in the roadway, and as she went she turned up the collar of the overcoat she had snatched off the row of hooks in the passage, for the rain was dripping into her neck. It then occurred to her that the overcoat was not her own. She had taken her own hat, cramming it down as far as her eyebrows; but she had got the wrong coat. She investigated it: it was her brother's—Bertie's. This seemed to her to be an extremely good joke—and Bertie, too, was always so particular about his things. She felt quite disproportionately heartened by this occurrence, and as she thrust her hands into the pockets to keep them dry she pretended to herself that she was a man, to give herself additional courage; she even affected a masculine stride, and whispered to herself, "Lydia Protheroe. . . Richard Protheroe. . . who am I?" and she skipped two or three paces in her excitement and trepidation. There was a pipe in the pocket of the coat; she curved her fingers round its little friendly bowl, and for a minute she even took it out and stuck it in her mouth, sucking at it as she had seen Bertie do, but almost immediately she slipped it back again with a guilty air and the sense of having done something inordinately daring, grotesque, and improper. The extravagance of her adventure was indeed going to her head. She had been for so long enveloped in the cotton-wool of her family that to be free of it was, simply, incredible. No father, no mother, no Bertie, to madden her with their injunctions and their restrictions. She skipped again, another two or three paces. But in the meantime she had no idea of where she was going or of what she meant to do. This irresponsibility was all very well, this release very delightful, but from Lydia Protheroe masquerading down a dark wet street in her brother's overcoat, to Lydia Protheroe the proprietress of a flourishing theatrical business, with her name over the door and fat ledgers on her desk, was a far cry; and she had nowhere to sleep that night.

She turned towards the station. Where did the next train go to? There would she go, even if it carried her to Wick or Thurso. Since she had abjured all the common prudences, she would allow fate to decide for her hap-hazard: fate was a Bohemian, if ever there was one, overthrowing careful plans and disregarding probabilities—a random deity which must henceforth be her guide. Before very long, she reflected, scoffing, though a little uncertainly, at herself meanwhile, she would be ordering her life by the spin of a coin or the conjunction of the planets, since here she was already, with not ten minutes of liberty behind her, resigning her destination into the keeping of Bradshaw. She hurried on towards the station, huddled inside the coat that was much too big for her, frightened but indomitable: still pretending to herself that she was a man—a boy, rather, and such phrases as "He ran away to sea" kept flitting through her mind, inconsequent but vaguely inspiriting—and although she was thereby transporting herself into a world of pretence, she could not help feeling, with exultation, that she had discarded forever the world of true pretence, of casuistry and circumspection, growing richer, more emancipated by the exchange. Presently she stood upon the railway bridge, looking down upon the station, an etching in silver-point never by her forgotten. The rails were lines of polished silver, the low black sheds of the station were spanned by girders against a black and silver sky. Only a few yellow lights gave colour; and, high up, the light of a signal, like a high and isolated ruby, burned deep upon the wrack of the silver-rifted clouds.

V

The difficulties of life had not sobered her. On the contrary, as she disencumbered herself more and more from the oppression of the traditions in which she had been brought up, her mettle had risen with proportionate buoyancy. She soared, as the weights dropped from her. She fled from these realities with increasing determination into the realms of make-believe. In her worst moments—for there had been bad moments, hours in her career which would have seemed to anyone else unpromisingly dark, hours when dishonesty saddened and failure discouraged her—she could always say to herself, "I don't exist at all. There's no such person as Lydia Protheroe." And she thought of all the parish ledgers, serious and civic, in which the birth, baptism, and other *faits et gestes* of Lydia Protheroe ought properly to be recorded, and from which Lydia Protheroe was so gratifyingly absent. This habit of mind grew upon her, until every suggestion of her actual existence as a citizen and a ratepayer was enough to throw her into a state of indignation. Who was Lydia Protheroe, that unsubstantial and fantastic being, that she should be bound down to the orthodoxy of an urban district council form for the payment of property-tax or house-duty? that she should be asked to account for her income and to contribute a shilling in the pound towards the upkeep of her country? she who had no country, no status? she who was so impudently and audaciously a myth? It was manifestly impossible to induce the tax-collectors to take this view. It would have entailed, moreover, the betrayal of Lydia Protheroe's secret, and the asking of questions leading inevitably to the resurrection of Alice Jennings. She consoled herself, therefore, in the midst of her mortification as she filled in her forms (never until "third application" glared across the top of the paper), by reflecting that she was playing a trick on the authorities with her tongue well thrust into her cheek. But there was nothing she would not do to evade the census returns, when they came round in 1891, and again in 1901, and again in 1911.

VI

Her family had been quite wrong when they predicted a change in her appearance. The sleek brown bands remained the same, the snuff-coloured gown, though of necessity every few years it had to be replaced by a successor, to outward appearance was unaltered. Lydia Protheroe, inheriting an odd and incongruous remnant of Presbyterianism from the late Alice Jennings, considered freedom of the spirit of more consequence than eccentricity of garb. Therefore, her external sobriety gave no hint of her internal flamboyance. People used to remark that the only thing in the shop devoid of all fantasy was the proprietor behind the counter. "Proper Protheroe" they called her, and similar names. But they had to admit her supremacy on all questions of travesty. She had more than the mere technical, the mere historical, knowledge; she had a flair and an imagination which surprised and convinced, unarguably. Without a trace of enthusiasm she issued her directions, coldly pointing with a ladylike forefinger, and when the finger was not in use she resumed that characteristic, tight little attitude, which had remained with her, of clasping her elbows with the opposite hand, while she watched her directions slavishly carried out. Her customers wondered whether she was ever gratified by her complete success. If so, she never betrayed it. The utmost approval that she was known to bestow, was a chilly "That will do." And yet, after her forty years of labour, she was a recognized authority in her profession; hidden away in her provincial town, she was the court of appeal in all problems connected with her trade, an arbitrator to whom even London had recourse. People said that as time went on she became grimmer and more intimidating. Certainly she became more self-contained, and none knew what passed beneath the sleek brown bands in their unvariable neatness, or behind the gown that buttoned, like a uniform, down the front. Something of a legend grew up around the personality of Lydia Protheroe. It became the fashion for strangers in the town to pay a visit to the shop, buying a box of powder or a stick of lip-salve to provide themselves with an excuse, while they covertly observed the ambiguous gentlewoman. The legend gradually became enhanced by scraps of gossip that crept into circulation about Lydia Protheroe. It was known in the town that she no longer allowed her solitary servant to sleep in the house, but that at six o'clock punctually, when the staff of the shop, consisting of three, left the premises, the servant-girl went with them. The bell over the door would tinkle for the last time of the day, the three assistants, turning up their collars or burying their hands in their muffs, would issue out one by one into the street, the servant-girl bringing up the rear; three "Goodnight, Miss Protheroe's" would be rapped out, and one "Goodnight, miss," from the servant, always scared and never in the least devoted; and the door would be shut behind them, and there would be the sound of the key turning in the lock.

VII

Darkness and silence then descended on the house. In one of the upper rooms a light would appear behind the blind; a light which sometimes moved from room to room, as though someone were carrying it about; and it had been seen, also, in the shop through the chinks of the shutters. But, although the curious had often lingered round the door, no one had ever been seen to emerge after dark.

The face of the house and the closed door kept their counsel as to whatever might be enacted behind them. All that the town ever knew was that evening after evening Lydia Protheroe was undisturbed at her own occupations, and although it was improbable to imagine that occupations otherwise than innocent could engage the leisure of so decent and correct a lady, there grew up, nevertheless, an impression of some mischievous background to the frontage of honest trade which everyone was allowed to see.

Why did she remain in this insignificant town, she who both by wealth and repute was amply justified to move herself and her chattels to London? Why had she chosen this ancient house, with its latticed windows and overhanging gables in a narrow side-street, rather than one of the new buildings in the main street, where were the other shops that, unashamed, did not have to tuck themselves away? Why did she sleep there alone at nights, among her oddments that were enough, when the mystery of dusk began to shroud them, to give an ordinary Christian the shivers? Why did she hold herself so frigidly aloof from the conviviality of the town? Perfectly civil always, they would say that much for her; and quite the lady, they would say that too. And good to the poor; oh, absurdly! That was only another one of the grievances they had against her: she spoilt the market for everybody else. But why—the questions would begin again. There was a mutter of innuendo; and yet, when they were pinned down to it, there was not one of her fellow townsmen who could say that she was otherwise than harmless. And they were all afraid of her, although she never said a sharp word; and they all respected her, grudgingly, and admitted her rigid integrity. But when these admissions had been extracted from them, the questions and the mutter would begin again.

Nobody knew whether she herself was aware of them; if she was, then she treated them with complete indifference. In point of fact, her mental isolation was such that she had long since ceased to bother her head about what people might say or might leave unsaid; she imagined herself encased in armour like the knight who stood eternally on the lowest step of her stair. She was happy. If she was forbidding, it was because she wanted no intimacy; she wanted to keep her happiness to herself. There were moments when she even resented the intrusion of customers into her shop, and the presence of the three assistants and the servant, but she tried to be severe with herself over this crotchet. Generally her severity was successful; but sometimes her resentment gained the upper hand, and on those occasions she would observe her hirelings with real dislike, angry with them because they, poor souls, went innocently on with their business, turning over the wares in the course of serving customers, until Miss Protheroe, unable longer to endure the sight of their hands fumbling among the objects got together by her and so dear to her heart, descended upon them from behind the counting-desk and brushed them aside, not rudely, for Miss Protheroe was never rude, but with a thin disdain that was twice as humiliating. For years she was deeply ashamed after these manifestations; then she grew to be less ashamed, and they increased in frequency. She became, coldly, more autocratic; would not have anything touched without her permission; received any comment with a scornful disapproval that would not permit her to answer. She was happy, but she was only truly and completely happy after six o'clock, when she had turned the key in the lock and was left alone in the house.

And yet she had a weakness, an inconsistency; she fretted over the defection of her family.

It was absurd. She wanted independence, and she had got it, full measure, pressed down and running over. She had been glad. She had been unobserved, left alone to do the little daring, extravagant things which bubbled up so surprisingly from beneath that ladylike exterior, little things like pretending she was a boy in her brother's overcoat, and drawing his pipe from the pocket to put it between her teeth. She had always done them surreptitiously, even though she knew she was quite alone. Sometimes she had made up her face with her own grease-paints, and, to the light of her candle, minced round the shop in a wig and a bustle. These were not things she would have had the courage to do with her family in the neighbourhood. She had believed that she would shed her family quite lightly, blissfully, and for sometime she had even deluded herself into the conviction that this was so. Then she was forced to the realization that their conduct had, in fact, sunk very deeply into the tender parts of her being. This realization took a long time to come. She had her first misgivings when she found that she could not think of them without a surge of anger uneasily allied to a surge of pain. Their silence had surprised her extremely. Daily she had expected to have some news of them; she had expected that they would trace her out—nothing easier—and many times in her mind she rehearsed the scene when one of their number, probably Bertie, would appear in the doorway of the room, and turn by turn, menacing, cajoling, and alarmed, would try to persuade her to return. These persuasions she would reject; of that she had been fully determined. It was not that she hankered after forgiveness and the evening circle round the lamp; it was not that she had desired the rôle of the prodigal child, picturesque and doubly precious after her escapade; no, it was not that she had wanted her family, but rather that she had wanted her family to want her. And not that alone. It was not, as she told herself plaintively, merely the petty, personal grievance that had hurt her. It was a wider, deeper injury. She despised them—she was compelled to despise them—because of their miserable cautiousness, their rejection of her, who was of their own blood, when she became a danger to their respectability. How politic they had been! how sage! She hated them because they had made her ashamed of them. They had become, to her, symbolic of that wary, chary majority whose enemy she was.

For the appearance of Bertie, however, she had waited in vain. They had made no attempt to retrieve her, nothing to show that they cared whether she lived or died, starved or prospered. Her expectation had turned to surprise, surprise to indignation. When it had finally become quite clear that they intended to take no steps towards getting her back, she accepted their indifference with a shrug that she tried to make equally indifferent. But the sore had remained; more, it had eaten its way down into her. There was no affection left now; but before she died she would be even with them. It was not a sore that impaired her happiness. Rather she nursed it, as she nursed all the secrets of her inner life; and it provided an incentive, if she had needed one, a sort of aim and *raison d'être*. Not a day passed but she wondered whether they heard the name of the celebrated Lydia Protheroe, and connected it with that of the little Alice they had so improvidently driven from their midst. She hoped so; spitefully she hoped so. She even contemplated going to London, where her reputation would widen with more chance of reaching their ears; but she could not uproot herself from her old clandestine house. She loved it, for the sake of six o'clock and the turning of the key in the lock.

So she lived with her two passionate secrets side by side: her vindictiveness and her absorption in the unreality of her own existence. The one intensified the other. An outcast from the auspices of middle-class propriety, she was driven into the refuge of her queer fantastic world. She sought that refuge fanatically, it was a facet of her vindictiveness. From out of that world of shadows she should, some day, thrust the rapier of mischief into the paunch of their gross solidity. It was all a little confused in her mind. But she felt that she owned, by right of citizenship—unshared citizenship, and consequent sovereignty, a sovereignty like that of Adam in Eden—she felt that she owned those privileges which had always given to the hero of mythical combat an advantage so preponderatingly unfair and so divine: the cap of invisibility, the armour that no sword could pierce, the sword that could pierce all armour, the winged shoes, the nightingale for counsellor, the philtre of oblivion, the mirror of prophecy. And at night, flitting round her house or down into her shop, to the echo of her own low laughter, now masked, now sandalled, now casqued within a head incongruous to the body and more incongruous to the feet, like the unfolding in a game of drawing Consequences, she knew herself elusive, evanescent, protean.

But no one must know, no one must suspect.

VIII

It was on an evening in December that Bertie's letter came. She was alone in the shop when she heard the click of the letterbox, and, getting the letter out, she instantly recognized the writing, and her heart, for a second, ceased to beat. She stood holding the letter, incredulous, and strangely afraid. Without knowing in exactly what way the opportunity would come to her, she had never for one instant doubted that somehow or other it would come. She tore the flap and read:

My Dear Alice,

"It is now some forty years since that terrible and painful scene which ended in our separation, and I think you will agree with me that so many years should have sufficed to heal our differences. We are both, my dear sister, past the prime of our life, and it is my earnest wish (as I trust it may be yours also) that a reconciliation should sweeten the advent of old age. I write, therefore, to propose that we take advantage of this season of good-will to bury the feud which has so long severed us. Our father and mother, as you must be well aware, have long since gone to their rest; but I remain (an old fellow now), and my dear wife and Emily and her husband. Would you give us a welcome if we came to visit you this Christmas-tide? I will add no entreaty, but leave the rest to the dictates of your heart.

Your brother,
Albert

She recognized Bertie's style; he had always been partial to books. She was convulsed by an inward laughter. So they had got wind of her riches! So they had an eye on her will! So her prosperity might sanction, at last, her discreditable trade! Would she welcome them, indeed? They should see how she would welcome them. Bertie, his wife, Emily, her husband—that would make four. She would have them all. There was plenty of room, fortunately, in the old house upstairs. She would have them on Christmas-eve. For a clear day, Christmas-day, she would have them to herself; all to herself! Her mind worked rapidly. She sat perched on a stool beside the counter, nibbling the tips of her fingers and making her plans. Her excitement was such that she found it difficult to keep the plans in her head consecutive; but she knew it was urgent that she should do so; she grabbed back her intentions as they tried to evade her. The envelope—Bertie had addressed her as "Miss Lydia Protheroe." He must have winced as he saw himself confronted by the necessity of writing that name. Bertie must be sixty-five now; Emily must be fifty-nine. So Emily had married—the little sister; she had always been a sly, mercenary little thing. Emily, Bertie, Bertie's wife—they all rushed back to her in their old familiarity. Bertie must have grown very like his father; she hated the implication of continuance. *Natura il fece, e poi roppe la stampa*; that was not the case with people like her father and Bertie. They were always the same. Their moral timidity extended itself into physical plagiarism. What would Emily's husband be like? All sugar to the rich sister-in-law, well-primed by the rest of the family. She let out a shrill of laughter. She would get them all into the house. She would put up the shutters and turn the key, and her Christmas entertainment would begin.

IX

They arrived in response to her invitation, on Christmas-eve, all four of them, driving up in the station fly, Bertie on the box. She stood on the doorway, awaiting them, and "Lydia Protheroe, Theatrical Costumier and Wig-maker," flaunted over her head in the gilt lettering on the black ground. She was conscious of her exquisite disparity with this description. Sleek bands, and snuff-coloured gown; Bertie and Emily should find her as they had left her; the difference should only by degrees dawn upon them. She was glad now that she should have rejected the alteration in her appearance which, to a less subtle mind, would have been so blatantly indicated. There was nothing blatant about Lydia Protheroe; oh no! it was all very surreptitious, very delicate; she was an artist; everybody said so; her touch very light, but very certain. She was a rapier to Bertie's bludgeon. Bertie: he had descended from the fly, he had taken both her hands in his, he had grown whiskers like his father's, his father's watch-chain (she recognized it) spanned his stomach, he was pressing her hands and looking into her eyes with what she was sure he inwardly phrased as "a world of tenderness and forgiveness," while simultaneously he tried to scan out of the corner of his eye the wares displayed in her shop-window—the dragon's head, the waxen figure of a fairy, the crowns and harps—and she saw him wince, but at the same time, she saw his determination to ignore all this, or to accept it, if he was forced to, in a spirit of jovial resignation; and now Emily was kissing her, Emily with those same thin ungenerous lips and pointed nose, so like her own features and yet so different, because of a recklessness in Lydia's eyes which was not in Emily's—subtle again— and now Bertie's wife enveloped her in a soft, fat little hug; and there was Emily's husband, whom they called Fred, and who was a pink-faced little man in a bowler hat and, for some reason, an evening tie, pushed forward to embrace his sister-in-law with a reluctance he tried to turn into enthusiasm.

Lydia brought the brood into the shop; it gave her a strange pang to see them cross her threshold, succeeded by an exaltation to have got them safely there. She did not talk much; she let them do the talking while she surveyed them. Bertie was voluble; he had a lot of information to give her, mixed in with small outbursts of sentimentality. He had grown portly, and he was most anxious to conciliate her; she took the measure of Bertie in a moment. The others, clearly, were in his charge. His wife, as ever, watched him for her cues with little twinkling, admiring eyes. Emily produced a sour and unconvincing smile whenever Lydia's eyes rested on her. As for Fred, he smiled nervously the whole time, and looked as though he felt himself very much of a stranger.

X

She had got them all into their rooms for the night. She relished the feeling that she had got them all safely shut in, and as she stood at the top of the stairs looking first to left and then to right along the dim passage, she felt the jailer of all those four people behind the closed doors. She would have liked a bunch of keys dangling from her belt. Squeezing her hands tightly together, she swayed backwards and forwards as she controlled her laughter. A single gas-jet, turned low, lit the passage. She wandered away. She wandered down into the shop, where the polished shields on the walls threw back the sharp flame of her candle, and the indistinct, peopled obscurity of the shop. She thought vaguely that the shop was too full—had always been too full—she must have a clearance—but there was no longer any room upstairs—she ought to scrap half her things—but no, they were too precious. She wandered away again, up into the attic. She peered round, thrusting the candle into the dark corners. A rat scurried past. Old trunks, too full to shut; velvet and damask and leather protruded; too full. Like life; too full. Like her head; too full. She wandered back to the dim passage. Closed doors. The gas-jet. She could turn off the gas at the main; that would put the house in darkness. They would not understand what had happened. They would run out of their rooms, and up and down the house, looking for light; finding none; blundering against objects in the dark. She would hear their footsteps, running; their hands, perhaps, beating at last upon the shutters. She had seen clearly enough that they already thought her strange. She had accompanied Bertie and his wife to their rooms, and under her scrutiny they had continued their talk; they had drawn a picture of the social life in their town; they had spoken of nice little parties. "Not so nice as the little party I'm giving now," Lydia had cried, and left them.

Husband and wife indeed thought her very odd; the wife was puzzled and uneasy. All through dinner Miss Protheroe had been very silent, from her place at the head of the table where she sat surveying her guests, only occasionally she had given vent to some such outburst, which she had at once restrained; and the dining-room had been odd too, a room at the back of the shop, full of queer theatrical things, and a great figure of a Javanese warrior in one corner, seven feet high, with a bearded yellow mask under his helmet, and a lantern swinging from the top of the spear he held in his hand. Bertie's wife thought this a novel and unpleasing method of lighting a room. She had begun to wish they had never come. For the rest, there had been a barbaric flavour about the meal, unsuitable to one so obviously an English spinster; they had eaten off the sham gold plate, and had drunk out of the sham gold goblets; the sham gold candelabra had flared in the middle of the table with its eight or ten candles, above a great golden bowl of artificial fruit.

It was difficult to believe that that setting was the invention of Lydia, sitting there so prim in the unchanged gown of bombazine. It was as disconcerting an indication as if Lydia had gotten up and danced.

Out in the dim passage Lydia paused before Emily's door. If she despised Bertie, she fairly hated Emily. Not one of Emily's childish sneakings and whinings was forgotten; and Emily was unchanged: she had been dragged here, reluctant, by Bertie, tempted by the pictures Bertie drew of Lydia's wealth; unable to resist that, she had come, but she was bitter and ungracious, wringing out that thin, sour little smile whenever Lydia looked at her. That supposed wealth, now become one of Lydia's dearest jokes! They wouldn't find much—the vultures—they would find that Lydia hadn't hoarded, hadn't kept back more than the little necessary to her own livelihood, so long as charity had stretched out to her its piteous hands. It was not part of Lydia's creed to feast while others went hungry. Not for that had she broken away from her traditions and her family. She would have liked now to sham dead just for the sake of seeing their faces and hearing their comments.

She wasted no time on Emily; she needed no sight of Emily's face in order to whet her vindictiveness. She knew well enough what was going on behind all those closed doors. Whispers of cupidity, to the ugly accompaniment of the calculation of Lydia's prosperity, oh, she knew, she knew! Mean souls! mean, prudent souls! They had thrown her out when she was poor; they fawned on her now that they thought her rich. Well, she would teach them a lesson; she would give them twenty-four hours' entertainment which they would not be likely to forget.

She crept away, down the dark stairs into her shop. At home again, among her fanciful and extravagant confederates! She held out her arms towards her shop, as though to embrace it. They were allies, she and it, the world of illusion against the world of fact.

She set to work.

XI

Next morning her guests came down to breakfast with white faces. They shot doubtful glances at Lydia when she blandly wished them a happy Christmas. There were parcels put ready for them beside all their plates, and Lydia observed with sarcasm their reviving spirits as they opened them in optimistic expectancy, and their consternation as they discovered the contents: a big, pink turned-up nose for Bertie, a blue wig for Bertie's wife, a pair of ears for Fred, and a black moustache for Emily. Led by Bertie, they tried at first to disguise their vexation under good-humour:

"Ha! ha! very funny, my dear," said Bertie, putting on the nose and poking it facetiously into his wife's face.

"But you must all put them on," said Miss Protheroe, without a smile.

They looked at her: she was perfectly serious and even compelling. They began to be a little afraid, though they were even more afraid of showing it. They tried to expostulate, still good-humouredly, but, "If you don't like my presents, you can't eat my breakfast," said Miss Protheroe.

They had to comply. Lydia presided gravely, while the four sat round the table, eating kippers, tricked out in their respective presents. Emily, whose black moustache worked up and down as she ate, was controlled only by the beseeching gaze of Bertie's eyes over the top of the enormous nose; Bertie's wife shed silent tears which fell into her plate.

"Shall you expect us, my dear," Bertie said towards the end of that grim meal, feeling that it was becoming urgent to break the silence, "to go to church like this?"

"Church? you aren't going to church," replied Lydia.

There was a chorus: Not go to church on Christmas-day?

"No," said Lydia; "but," she added suddenly, "you can give me your offertory, and I'll see that it reaches the proper quarter. Charity at Christmas time! Turn out your pockets."

"Look here, Alice," said Bertie, standing up, "this is going beyond a joke. Be very careful, or we shall be obliged to leave your house."

"You can't," said Miss Protheroe. "The doors are locked, the shutters are locked and barred, and you stay here for as long as I choose to keep you. You are my guests—see? And I've waited for you, for forty years. I shan't let you go now."

They heard her words; they stared at one another with a sudden horror leaping in their eyes.

XII

B ertie's wife began to weep, loudly and helplessly.

"Oh, let me get out of this," she cried; "why did we ever come? Bertie, it was your fault. Oh, why didn't you leave her alone? the wicked, mad woman? Think of the noises in the night. The house haunted, and Alice mad! For God's sake let's clear out."

"She's in league with the Devil," said Emily in the black moustache.

They had all forgotten, by now, about the appearance they variously presented, and all stared at each other fearfully, grotesque, ridiculous, but unheeding.

"Christmas morning!" cried Bertie's wife, and wept more bitterly than before.

"Here, I've nothing to do with this—*I* never turned you out," said Fred to Lydia, speaking for the first time.

"You haven't given me your offertory yet," said Lydia. "Now then," she said, "out with it! Bertie, you used to be a churchwarden at home; you take round the plate."

Bertie's wife screamed when she saw a revolver in Lydia's hand.

"Keep quiet, you women!" said Bertie, playing the male; "if she's mad, we must humour her. Where's your money?"

They fumbled, the two men in their pockets, the two women in their bags, not one of them daring to take their eyes off Lydia for an instant.

"Is that all you've got?" asked Lydia, when the plate presented by Bertie was filled with silver, copper, and notes; "turn out the linings." They obeyed. "You may go to your rooms now, if you like," she added, "but don't be late for dinner; we'll have it at one. And mind you come down as you are now. You're no more disguised like that, let me tell you, than you are with your every-day faces. There's no such thing as truth in you, so one disguise is no more of a disguise than any other. Your shams are just as much shams as my shams. And that's one of the things you can learn while you're here."

They filed out of the room, past the tall figure of Lydia, who, like a grim grenadier, watched them go, still perfectly grave, but with an awful mockery in her eyes. She savoured to the full the absurdity of their appearance. There was no detail of incongruity which escaped her glance. When they had all got out of the room, and she had heard them scurrying, frightened rabbits, up the stairs, she sat down again in her chair and laughed and laughed. But it was not quite the wholesome laugh of one who plays a successful practical joke; it was, rather, a cackle of real malevolence, the malevolence that has waited and brooded and been patient, that has dammed up its impulse for many years. She sat and laughed at the head of her table, with the debris of the brown paper parcels strewn beside every plate.

D own to dinner under the threat of the revolver. She was intolerant now of the smallest resistance. She got them sitting there in the same travesty, forced them to eat, forced them to entertain her with their conversation. "No glum faces!" she said sharply. It was hard enough to look glum under those additions to nature; Bertie's nose especially had a convivial air, it imposed upon him a gross jollity he was very far from feeling. They ate turkey and plum-pudding, unwillingly, choking back, according to their natures, their fury or their tears. Lydia had not stinted their fare; but then, she had never been niggardly. There was a lavishness in her providing; there were raisins, almonds, brandy; and she urged the appetites of her guests with an ironical though genuine hospitality. "Christmas dinner, you know," she said to them as she heaped the food upon their plates. They protested; she nearly laughed at the piteous protest in their eyes shining out through their ridiculous trappings. But she remembered the forty years, and the laughter died unborn.

Forty years—and she had got them to herself. She would let them off nothing.

XIV

After dinner they huddled all four together in the same room. They could not lock themselves in, because Lydia had removed all the keys.

They whispered together a good deal, running up and down the scale from apathy to indignation. They had even moments of curiosity, when they ferreted among the hotch-potch of things they found stuffed away in the cupboards and drawers, and under the bed; and speculated marvelling on the queerness of Alice's existence among these things: forty years of masquerade! But for the most part they sat gloomy, or wandered aimlessly about the room, dwelling in their own minds upon their several apprehensions. Bertie's wife said, "It's all so vague—only hints, so to speak," and a background of shadows leapt into being.

Steps prowled past in the passage; they prowled up and down. The four in the room looked at one another. There was a faint cry outside, and a laugh.

"Two people, or one?" they whispered.

There was no telling how many people the house might conceal. The resources of the shop alone could transform Lydia into a hundred different characters. She would change her personality with each one. They could not contemplate this idea. It credited her with uncanny powers. Their imaginations, which had never in their lives been set to work before, now gaped, pits full of possibilities.

They peeped and were afraid.

Towards four o'clock it grew dark and they lit the gas, but after an hour or so it suddenly went out. They could not find any matches, hunting round in the dark. "Is there no light?" said their voices. Somebody found the door, opened it, and fled out: it was Fred. They heard him running down the passage, and his steps upon the stair. He would get down into the shop; he must look after himself. They sat down in the dark, pressed together to listen and to wait.

XV

It was the silence in the house, all that afternoon and evening, which frightened them. They were left to themselves, there was no sign of Lydia; there was no sound in the house but the sounds they made themselves. Now and then one of them would get up and go restlessly over to the window: but though they debated whether they should hail a passer-by in the street they feared too greatly the consequences of the scandal. Whatever happened, this thing must remain a secret forever; on that point they were agreed and decided. This consideration kept them from the violence they might otherwise have attempted. No one must know. . . poor Lydia. . . her shame was their shame. . . madness in the family. . . So they kept silent; meekness was the only prudence. Weary, they realized that they were old, and looked at one another with a kind of pity. They spoke very little. Their lives stretched out behind them, enviable in their secure monotony. Never had they envisaged the grotesque as a possible element. The only grotesque that had had a place in their minds, was death; and that, by virtue of much precedent, was sanctioned into conformity.

"She's got the better of us," said Emily once.

"No, no, no," said Bertie with sudden energy; he could not admit it. "No, no," he said again, getting up and walking about. "*No*," he said, striking with his fist into the palm of the other hand.

They waited till the evil hours should have passed and the normal be reasserted.

XVI

There remained the evening and the night. Lydia had said Christmas-day, and for some reason they took for granted that after Christmas-day was passed all would be over—one way or the other. The shutters would be unbarred, the shop reopened, and life would return to the cloistered house. Still the evening and the night. What a Christmastide! And they were old; too old for such pranks. Bertie was sixty-five. Old, too old. They were tired of the strain of the silent day. Hungry, too, although they had not noticed it. They went downstairs meekly when Lydia summoned them to supper. Nose, ears, moustache, blue wig; no attempt at rebellion. They sat round the table, waiting to be given their food and drink. They had half hoped that Lydia would present some unexpected appearance; if she was mad, she ought to look mad; that would be less terrifying. It was horrible to be so mad and to continue to look so sane. She might have been an old family governess; a strict one. Whereas they were condemned to sit there, so ludicrous; knowing, moreover, that she lost none of the full savour of the paradox.

"You shall drink my health," she said, at the opening of the meal.

They drank it, in neat spirit. She plied them with more.

"I never touch anything," said Emily feebly.

"No, but this is an exception." She poured freely into Emily's glass, drinking nothing herself.

The Javanese warrior holding the lantern on his spear grinned down at them with his yellow mask. The candles flickered in the great sham candelabras. The spirit was tawny in the shining glasses.

"Drink! it's our last evening together."

Emily looked at Lydia, they were sisters; had the same features; were not unlike one another.

"We shared a bedroom, Alice, didn't we? I got into your bed once, when I was frightened at night. There was a box made of shells on the dressing-table, do you remember? Mother gave it to us at the seaside."

She laughed; her laugh was almost tender.

"I used to pull your hair, Alice," said Bertie.

They were suddenly confident that Alice would do them no harm.

"Forty years," said Lydia, looking down the table at them.

"A waste of time," said Bertie, "when we were brother and sisters together. But you've paid us out, Alice, you've paid us out."

"Not yet," said Lydia, "not fully."

"I daresay I should have done the same myself," said Bertie's wife, surprisingly. "After all, it was a joke, Alice; why not take Alice's joke in good part?" She looked round, as though she had made a discovery.

"If you prefer," said Lydia, unmoved.

"Ha, ha!" said Fred, and was suddenly silent.

They began to eat what Lydia had given them. Beyond the open door of the dining-room the shop was dark and jumbled. Lydia ate primly, and the little black revolver lay beside her plate. The light glinted along its barrels. They viewed it without apprehension. This was their last evening; they were confusedly sorry; Alice, hospitable if eccentric; and what, indeed, was eccentricity? She was giving them champagne now; it was wrong to begin with spirits, and to go on to champagne; but what matter? Alice was well-meaning; generous. That little revolver: like a little black, shining bull-terrier, squat, bulbous. They heard themselves laughing and making jokes. Alice seemed pleased, she was smiling; up to the present she had not smiled at all; but now the smile was constant on her face as she watched them. They exerted themselves to entertain her. Their efforts were successful; she watched them with evident approval, swaying a little, backwards and forwards, as she sat. They ventured more; still she smiled, and her hand poured generously, though she did not empty her own glass. They had forgotten that they were old. Looking at one another, they laughed very heartily over the trappings Alice had provided for them. "Christmas!" said Bertie, tapping his nose. Emily leant back in her chair; she was sleepy and happy. She roused herself to accept the sweets which Lydia offered her. "Sleepy," she murmured, smiling at Bertie's wife; "your hair. . ." she toppled off to sleep in the midst of her sentence. Fred wanted to prop her up. "Let her be," said Lydia benignly. "All happy," said Bertie. They pulled crackers, and put the paper caps on their heads; the table under the candelabra was littered with the coloured paper off the crackers, and there was a discord produced by the whistles and small trumpets that came out of them. Bertie was on his feet, trying all these toy instruments in turn; he swayed round the table, collecting them, and reading out the mottoes. He paused to look at his wife, who had fallen forward with her arms on the table and her head on her arms. "Asleep," he said, with a puzzled expression. Lydia still sat bolt upright at the head of the table, letting them all have their way as it seemed best to them, whether in sleep or hilarity; with her hands she clasped her elbows, and the bands of hair lay undisturbed upon her brows. She examined her guests in turn; Emily, who slept, slipped sideway in her chair, the moustache still stuck on her upper lip; Bertie's wife, who slept likewise, her face hidden, the blue wig uppermost; Fred, who between the ears stared vaguely before him; and Bertie, who, portly and irresponsible, wandered round the table searching among the litter of the crackers. Lydia at last, having scrutinized them all, gave out a sudden creaking laugh. Her party was to her satisfaction. "Forty years!" she said, nodding at Bertie, "forty years!" When she laughed he looked at her, dimly startled through his confusion. "Christmas," he replied, blinking; he intended it to be an expression of good-will, an obliteration of those forty years. At last, he thought, they had found out the right way to treat Alice: not solemnly, not as though they were afraid of her, but in a light-hearted and jocund spirit. "Christmas," he repeated, leaning up against her chair.

She began to laugh. Her laughter grew; it creaked at first, then grew shrill; she pointed derisively at them all in turn. Bertie was not alarmed; he joined in. He relished at last the humour of the situation, which Alice had been relishing now since yesterday. She had got twenty-four hours' start ahead of him: an unfair advantage. He made up for lost time by trying to laugh more heartily than she did. She observed this with a dangerous appreciation; her fingers began to play with the butt of the revolver. Forty years. Forty Christmases spent in solitude. Her sudden rage blackened out the room before her eyes. She lifted the revolver uncertainly, then laid it down again. "Subtle, subtle. Not blatant," she muttered to herself, an often-rehearsed lesson, and tapped her fingers against her teeth. She felt slightly helpless, as though she were unable to make the most of her opportunity. She knew she had had many schemes, but they all seemed to be slipping away from her. It was difficult to hold on to one's thoughts, difficult to concentrate them; they scattered as one came up to them, like a lot of sparrows. A pity—she must make an effort—because the opportunity would not come again.

Just then she heard the front-door bell ring sharply through the house.

A little dazed, she got up to answer it. A messenger from outside? Perhaps an unexpected help in her emergency? She left the dining-room, where Bertie fumbled and tried to detain her; she passed through the shop, and, moving like a sleep-walker, unlocked and undid the many fastenings of the door. Outside in the street stood a group of men, carrying lanterns; the snow sparkled on the ground; the narrow street was like an illustration of old-fashioned Christmas. She stood holding the door open. She recognized many of her fellow-tradesmen; she heard their words, "Your well-known charity, Miss Protheroe. . . never turn away an appeal unanswered. . . Christmas-time. . . trust we don't intrude. . ." and heard the rattle of coin, and saw the collecting-boxes in their hands.

"You don't intrude," she said. "Come in."

Inwardly she knew they wanted an excuse to find out how Miss Protheroe spent her Christmas. They should see. They came in, removing their hats, from which the melting snow began to drip, and scraping the snow from their boots on the wire mat; their faces were red and jovial. She led them through the jumbled shop, through into the dining-room, where Bertie leant up against the littered table, and the two women slept, and Fred gaped stupidly.

They were at a loss to say anything; checked in their joke of routing out old Miss Protheroe, they gazed uncomprehending at the scene before them. Their eyes turned again towards Miss Protheroe; she stood erect and prim, her hands clasping her elbows.

"You don't know my relations," she said, and, indicating them, "my sister, my brother-in-law, my sister-in-law, my brother." She effected the introduction with irreproachable gravity.

"She's mad," cried Bertie suddenly, reason flooding him, and he pointed at her with a denouncing hand.

They stared, first at those four crazy figures, and then at the stiff correctness of Miss Protheroe as they always knew her.

PATIENCE

I

He had only to seclude his mind in order to imagine himself in the train again, to hear its steady beat, and to sway monotonously with its rocking. As soon as he had isolated himself in this day-dream, he was impervious to the sights and sounds that washed round on the outskirts of his consciousness. He was safely withdrawn. He sat staring, not at the green baize of the card-table, where his wife, with white, plump, be-ringed hands, under the strong light thrown down by the shaded lamp, set out the neat rows of shiny cards for her Patience; he sat staring, sheltered within the friendly shadows, not at this evening security of his home, but out through the rectangular windows of the train, that framed the hard blaze of the southern country, the red rocks and the blue sea; the train curving in and out of tunnels, round the sharp promontories, disclosing the secrets of little bays, the pine-trees among the boulders, and the blackened scrub that betokened a previous hillside fire.

Opposite him, *she* slept, curled up in the corner of the seat, very young and very fragile under the big collar of soft fur of her coat thrown over her to keep off the dust. He had wished that she would look out of the window with him; he knew how she would sit up, and the quick impatient gesture by which she would dash the hair out of her eyes, but she slept so peacefully, so like a child, that he would not wake her. He bent forward, knocking the ash of his cigarette off against the window-ledge, to get a better view out of the window; and every little creek, as the curving train took it out of view, he pursued with regretful eyes, knowing that he would not pass that way again. This forlorn and beautiful coast, whose every accident was so faithfully followed by the train, this coast, every bit of it, was a party to his happiness, and he had been reluctant to let it go.

How his heart ached! Perhaps it was not wholesome to have trained his mind to enter so readily, so completely, into that world of recollections? He dragged himself out:

"Patience going well?"

"Not very well tonight."

He drifted away again, before he well knew that he had drifted. Not to the train this time—his memories were illimitably various. (The time had been when he could not trust himself to dip into them, those memories that were now perpetually his refuge, his solace, and his pain.) An hotel bedroom. What hotel?—it didn't matter. All hotel bedrooms were alike; all Paradise, so long as they had contained *her*. In what spot?—that didn't matter, either; somewhere warm and gaudy; all their escapades had been in southern places. Somewhere with bougainvillæa ramping over creamy houses, somewhere with gay irresponsible negroes selling oranges out of immense baskets at the street corners. She had never tired of the gash of their white teeth in their black faces as they grinned. She would stop to buy their oranges just to get the grin. And some of them could juggle with oranges, which made her laugh and turn to him in delight and clap her hands. He clenched his fingers together, out of sight, as he lounged in the depths of his arm-chair. That hotel bedroom! Her clothes. . . He used to kneel on the floor beside her open dressing-case, lifting out her clothes for her, because she was too lazy to unpack for herself. She watched him through her eye-lashes, amused at his complaints which so ill concealed his joy in her possessions; then she would catch his head and strain it hungrily against her. They were always violent, irresistible, surprising, those rare demonstrations of hers, and left him dizzy and abashed. That hotel bedroom! Always the same furniture; the iron bedstead under the draped mosquito curtains that were so oddly bridal; the combined wash-stand and chest of drawers (the drawers incorrigibly half-open and spilling the disorder of her garments, her ribbons, and her laces), the hanging wardrobe with the long looking-glass door, the dressing-table littered with her brushes, her powder, and her scent bottles. The evenings—he would come noiselessly into her room while she lingered at her mirror, in her long silk nightgown, her gleaming arms lifted to take the pins out of her hair; and after standing in the doorway to watch her, he would switch off the electric light, so that the open window and the dark blue sky suddenly leapt up, deep, luminous, and spangled with gold stars behind her. Then the coo of her voice, never startled, never hasty: a coo of laughter and remonstrance, rather than of displeasure; and he would go to her and draw her out on to the balcony, from where, his arm flung round her shoulders and her suppleness yielding contentedly to his pressure, they watched the yellow moon mount up above the sheaves of the palm-trees, and glint upon a shield of distant water.

And there were other nights: so many, he might take his choice amongst them. Carnival nights, when she fled away from him and became a spirit, an incarnation of carnival, and the sweep of her dancing eyes over his face was vague and rapid, as though he were a stranger she had never seen before. He used to feel a small despair, thinking that any domino who whirled her away possessed her in closer affinity than he. And when he had at last thankfully brought her back into her room at the hotel, with confetti scattered over the floor, fallen from her carnival clothes, whose tawdry satin and tinsel lay thrown across a chair, then, although he could not have wished her sweeter, she still kept that will-o'-the-wisp remoteness, that air of one who has strayed and been with difficulty recaptured, which made him wonder whether he or anyone else would ever truly touch the secret of her shy and fugitive heart.

"How funny you are, Paul. You haven't turned over a page of your book for at least twenty minutes." Not a rebuke—merely a placid comment. Another set of Patience nicely dealt out.

After that he turned the pages assiduously, it wouldn't do to be caught dreaming. Then came the relapse. . .

She had flitted away from him; yes, the day had come when she had flitted. He had known, always, somewhere within himself, that it would come. To whom had she gone?—he didn't know; he hadn't tried to find out, perhaps to no one; and, anyway, the fate of her body, passionately as he had loved it, didn't seem so vital a matter; what mattered was the flame within her; he couldn't bear to think that she should have given anyone *that*. Not that he was fatuous enough to suppose that he had ever had it. Oh, no!—he was far too humble, too diffident in his mind. He had worshipped her all the more because he knew there was something in her withdrawn, the eternal pilgrim, the incorrigible truant. He knew that he could never have loved any woman who hadn't that element in her, and since he had only found it once, quite logically he had never loved but once. (He had been young then. It had been easy enough for his relations to pick holes in her: "Flighty," they had said, and, snorting, "She takes the best years of his life and then throws him aside," and to all their comments he had never answered once, but had looked at them with deeply wounded eyes, so that they wondered uneasily what thoughts were locked in his heart. Nor had they ever got any information out of him; all their version of the story had been pieced together from bits of gossip and rumour; correct in the main as to facts, but utterly at sea as to essentials. But as he disdained to set them right, they were never any the wiser.) Never loved but once; and here he was, fifty, prosperous, even envied by other men, going daily about his affairs, dining well, talking rationally, a certain portliness in his manner which his figure had escaped. . . He and his wife, a commendable couple; a couple that made one disbelieve in anarchy, wild oats, or wild animals. People smiled with the satisfaction of approval when they came into a room; here were security, decorum; here were civilization and politeness; here was a member of the civic corporation, a burgher to admire and to respect. He had a grave, courtly manner, slightly indulgent towards women, which they found not unattractive, although they knew that he varied it towards none of them, whether plain or pretty, staid or skittish. There was always the same grave smile on his lips, always the same sustained, controlled interest in his eyes; attention, perhaps, rather than interest; the line was a difficult one to draw. The type of man who made other men say, "Wish we had more fellows like him," and of whom the women said amongst themselves, "A puzzling man, somehow, isn't he? So quiet. One never knows what he is really thinking, or whether he isn't laughing at us all. Do you suppose, though, that he has ever really *felt*?"

The madcap things she did! He recalled that evening at the railway station, when under the glare of the arc-lights she had danced up to a ticket-collector—she in her little travelling hat and her furs and the soft luxury that always seemed to surround her: "When does the next train start?" "Where for, miss?" "Oh, it doesn't matter where for—just the next train?" And they had gone to Stroud.

"This Patience never seems to come out," said the voice proceeding from under the lamp.

"No, dear?"

"No. I think I shall have to give it up for an easier one. It's so irritating when things won't go right."

"I should try an easier one tomorrow."

"Tomorrow? Oh, I see, you want to go to bed. I must say, I should rather have liked to try it this evening, but if you want to go to bed. . ."

"No, dear, of course not; try your Patience by all means."

"No, dear; I wouldn't dream of it, as you want to go to bed. Besides, tomorrow will do just as well. You will go round, won't you, and see that everything is properly locked up?"

"But I am dragging you to bed when you don't want to go."

"Not a bit, Paul, I assure you; it is quite all right. I am really quite sleepy myself. I should have liked to try the Patience, perhaps, but tomorrow will do just as well."

He held the door open gravely for her, but there were several things she must attend to before leaving the room: the fire must be poked down so that no spark could be spat out on to the hearth-rug; the drawer of her writing-table must be locked so that the housemaid should not read her letters or examine her bills when dusting the room before breakfast on the following morning; and the book which she had been reading must be replaced in the bookcase. He endured all this ritual without betraying any irritation, watching even the final pats which she gave to the cushions of his chair.

"It's quite all right, Paul, dear; of course one can't help crumpling cushions when one sits on them, and what are they there for but to be sat on?"

She bustled out of the room, calling back to him as she mounted the stairs: "You won't forget to lock up, will you?"

He had remembered to lock up now for twenty years. He went methodically about the business, looking behind curtains to see whether the shutters were closed, testing the chain on the front door. All that paraphernalia of security! He felt sometimes that the cold, the poor, and the hungry were welcome to the embers of his drawing-room fire, to the silver off his sideboard, and to the remains of the wine in his decanters. And as he stood for a moment at the garden door, looking up the gravel path of his trim little garden, and felt the biting cold beneath the slip of new moon, he wondered with a sort of anguish where *she* was, whether she was sheltered and cared for, or whether in her gay improvident way she had gone down and under, until on such a winter's night as this there remained no comfort for her but such as she might find among the mirrors and garish lights of a bar, in such fortuitous company as she might charm with a vivacious manner and an affectation of laughter. She had from time to time been haunted by a premonition of such things, he remembered; a mocking wistfulness had come into her voice when she said, "You'll always be all right, Paul, you were born prosperous; but as for me, I'll end my days among the dregs of the world—I know it, so think of me sometimes when you sit over your Madeira and your cigar, won't you? and wonder whether my nose isn't pushed against your window in the hopes that the smell of your cooking might drift out to me," and when she had said these things he had put his hand over her mouth to stop the words he couldn't bear to hear, and she had laughed and had repeated, "Well, well, we'll see."

He shut the door carefully and shot the bolt into its socket. Very cold it was—silly of him to stand at the open door like that—hoped he hadn't got a chill. Lighting his candle in the hall, he switched off all the electric lights and climbed the stairs to bed; a nice fire warmed his dressing-room, and his pyjamas were put out for him over the back of a chair in front of the fire; he undressed, thinking that he was glad he wasn't a poor devil out in the cold. His wife was already in bed, and by the light of her reading-lamp he saw the curlers that framed her forehead, and the feather-stitching in white floss-silk round the collar of her flannel nightgown.

"What a long time you've been, Paul. I was just thinking, I shan't be able to try that Patience tomorrow evening, because we've got the Howard-Ellises coming to dinner."

"So we have. I'd quite forgotten. We must give them champagne," he said mechanically; "they'll expect it."

He got into bed, turned out the lamp, and lay down beside his wife, staring into the dark.

HER SON

To H. M.

I

She awoke that morning earlier than was her wont, emerging from a delicious sleep into a waking no less pleasant. Lazily she slipped her hand under her pillows—there were a lot of pillows, all very downy, into which her head and shoulders sank as into a nest; she liked a lot of pillows; that was one of her little luxuries, and she was in the habit of saying, what was one's own house if not a place where one's little luxuries could be indulged?—lazily she slipped her hand under the pillows, feeling about, and having found what she wanted, pressed the spring of the repeater watch lying there tucked away. Its tiny, melodious chime came to her, muffled but distinct. Seven clear little bells; then two chimes for the half-hour; then five quick busy strokes; five-and-twenty minutes to eight. Five-and-twenty minutes still before she would be called. She lay contentedly on her back, with her arms folded beneath her head, watching the daylight increase through the short chintz curtains of her windows opposite. The chintz, a shiny one, was lined with pink; the light came through it, pink and tempered. She lay wondering whether she should get up to pull the curtains aside, but she was so comfortable, so softly warm, and in so pleasant a frame of mind, that she would not break the hour by moving. She had a little world inside her head today making her independent of the world outside. And besides, she knew so well what she would see, even did she make the effort and get up to pull the curtains; she would see what she had seen everyday for forty years, the barn with the orange lichen on the roof, the church tower, the jumbled roofs of the village, the bare beautiful limbs of the distant Downs; she knew it all, knew it with the knowledge of love; and yet, in spite of this intimate knowledge, she was frequently heard to remark that the country had always some new surprise, some gradation of light one had never seen before, so that one was always on the look out and one's interest kept alive from day today. The seasons in themselves constituted a surprise to which, in her five-and-sixty years of life, she had never grown accustomed; she forgot each beauty as it became replaced by a newer beauty; in the delight of spring she forgot the etched austerity of winter, and in winter she forgot the flowers of spring, so it was always with a naïve astonishment that she recognized the arrival of a new season, and each one as it became established seemed to her the best. A discovery took sometime before it settled itself into its place in the working of her mind, but, once there, it held with a gentle obstinacy, and, because there were not very many of these discoveries, none of them were very far away from the circling current of her thoughts. Nor was she eager for fresh acquaintances among her thoughts, anymore than for fresh acquisitions among her friends; just as she liked faces to be familiar, so she liked ideas to be well-tested and proven before she admitted them to the privilege of her intimacy; the presence of strangers was an inconvenience; good manners forbade little jokes from which strangers were excluded, little allusive or reminiscent smiles in which they could not share. It followed, logically enough—although she enjoyed the small, carefully-chosen dinner parties she gave once a fortnight on summer evenings—that she was really happiest alone with her house and garden, because, as she said, one never knows anybody so well as one knows oneself, and even one's most approved friends are apt to contradict or to disagree, or to advance unforeseen opinions; to disconcert, in fact, in a variety of ways impossible to the silent acquiescence of plants or furniture; and the one person whose constant companionship she would have chosen, had hitherto been absent.

She was perfectly happy now as she lay waiting for eight o'clock and the beginning of the day, agreeable anticipations floating in her mind as her eyes wandered over the comfort of her room, from the chintz curtains to the bright stoppered bottles and silver on her dressing-table, from the small bookcase full of nicely-bound books to the row of photographs on the mantelpiece. All was very still. One of the curtains bellied out a little in front of an open window. From time to time a smile hovered over her lips, and once she gave a sigh, and moved slightly in her bed, as though the very perfection of her thoughts were giving her a deliciously uneasy rapture. But she never allowed herself to indulge for long in reveries which, however pleasant they might be, led to nothing practical. She knew that she had a great deal to see to that morning; and if all were not done in an orderly way, something would be forgotten. She stretched out her hand and took from off the table by her bed a memorandum book, fitted with a pencil and bound in green leather, across which was written in gilt lettering, "*While I remember it.*"

With the pencil poised above the first fair page, she paused. Would it be better to execute her business in the village first, or to do what she had to do about the house? The village first, by all means; if any of the tradesmen made a mistake, there would be the more time to rectify

V. SACKVILLE-WEST

their blunder. She began, in her mind, her journey up the village street, stopping at the stationer's, the grocer's, the fishmonger's.

How difficult it was to cater for the wants of a man! So long since she had done it; she had lost the habit. What would he want? The *Times*. She noted "*Times*," and added, after a long concentration, "*The Field*." Then she remembered that he liked J pens; she herself always used Relief; how lucky that she had thought of that. There was nothing else from the stationer's; of all the ordinary requirements, writing-paper, blotting-paper, ink, pencils, gummed labels, elastic bands, envelopes of assorted sizes, she kept in her cupboard an exhaustive store. The grocer next; and she had already, a long way back, when she first heard that Henry was coming, made a note that he liked preserved ginger. She renewed this note, neatly, under the proper heading in her list: Ginger, Brazil nuts, a small Stilton, anchovies—he would want a savoury for dinner, and he should have it—chutney. She could not think of anything else, but once she was in the shop she could look round and perhaps see something that he would like. She passed on to the fishmonger's, and with a delighted smile wrote down, "Herring roes" and "Kippers." How amused and pleased he would be when he realized how well she had remembered all his tastes! Not the taste he had when he was a little boy, and which she might have remembered out of sentiment; no, he should see that she had kept pace with his years, and remembered his preferences as a man up to five years ago, when she had last seen him.

She had finished now with the village, for all the more staple requirements had, of course, been ordered at the beginning of the week, and these were only the extras which she had treasured up to do herself on the last morning. There was more to be seen to at home. Flowers— no, she need not make a note of that; she would not forget to do the flowers. But there were other things which, unless noted, might slip her memory:

"Order the motor; eggs (brown) for breakfast; honey; fire in his room; put out the port; put out the cigars; early morning tea."

At that moment she heard the church clock beginning to strike eight, and with a knock on the door her maid came in, carrying a little tray in one hand and a can of hot water in the other. There were a few letters slipped under the edge of the saucer on the tray, and Mrs. Martin read them while she drank her tea, but they were not very interesting, only the annual appeal from the local gardeners' society—she thought it unthrifty to send that by post, when it could so easily have been left by hand—a couple of bills, a bulb catalogue from Holland ("Early every morning will be seen dozens of parties of men, women and children tramping up the mountains between France and Spain, singing the popular song of Harry Lauder, 'We're all going the same way, we've all gone down the hills.' Now perhaps you will ask me why I tell this in a Bulb Catalogue, and here I will give you the answer: In the valleys of those beautiful Pyrenees mountains live numerous daffodils, which are the richest flowering of these garden-friends I ever meeted. Will you not try a couple of hundred from our stock? and you will be convinced to have invested fife bob on the good horse."), and a letter from her sister in Devon which she put aside to read later on. The maid moved about the room, putting everything ready very quietly and skilfully. The curtains were drawn back now, and from her bed Mrs. Martin could see the wide autumn sky, gold-brown behind the scarlet trail of splay-leaved Virginia creeper that hung down outside the window. She was glad that it was neither raining nor windy. She would have the motor opened before it started for the station.

The day had really begun.

A rising tide of excitement made her want very much to talk to Williams, but this was against her principles, and she restrained herself. She kept glancing at Williams whenever the maid's back was turned, or her head bent over the linen in the tidy drawers, and opening her lips to speak, but the remark faded away each time into a nervous smile, which she concealed by drinking again from her cup of tea. But when Williams came and stood by her bed to say, "The bath is quite ready, ma'am," she could not prevent herself from speaking; she wanted to say, "You know, it's today, Williams, today!" but instead of that she said, with detachment, "Is it a fine morning, Williams?" and Williams replied, respectful as ever, "A beautiful morning, ma'am," but Mrs. Martin, as she got out of bed and slid her feet into the warmed bedroom slippers that were waiting for her, felt that between herself and Williams a perfectly satisfactory understanding existed.

V. SACKVILLE-WEST

II

S he came downstairs in due course, dressed in a brown holland dress with a big black straw hat tied with black ribbons under her chin. Her fresh old face looked soft and powdered, her white hair escaped in puffs from under her hat, on her nose she wore a pair of round horn spectacles, and on her hands a pair of big brown leather gauntlets. Over her arm she carried a garden basket, a pair of garden scissors dangling by a ribbon from the handle. She was going to do the flowers first; one never knew, at this time of year, whether a sudden shower might not come down and dash their beauty.

In the hall, at the bottom of the stairs, the grandfather clock ticked quietly. The doors all stood open; looking to the left she could see into the sitting-room, with its deep, chintz-covered chairs and sofas; looking to the right, down the passage, into the dining-room, where presently luncheon would be laid for two; and straight ahead of her, facing the stairs, was the front door, which opened on to the little forecourt and the flagged path leading up to the porch. She went out. Some white pigeons were sunning themselves on the roof of the great barn; its doors were propped open, and a farm-hand came out, followed by two farm horses, their hoofs going clop-clop after him, their harness clanking loosely, and their blinkers and the high peaks of their collars studded with shining brass nails. Their tails and manes were plaited up with straw and red braid. Mrs. Martin nodded to the man, as he touched his cap to her, and stood looking after the horses lumbering their way out towards the lane. She liked having the farm so close at hand, and had never thought of putting the barn, although it stood so near the house, forming one side of the forecourt, to any other than farm uses. She went across the court now, and looked into it. A smell of dust and sacking; gold motes in a shaft of sunlight; two farm waggons with red and blue wheels; a pile of yellow straw, and some trusses of hay. She was very well content. Behind the barn stood the rickyard, and here were the garnered stacks, pointed like witches' hats, a double row of them: the farm was doing well. When the time came, she would have a prosperous inheritance to bequeath to her son.

She turned away from the shadows of the barn, and went through the door in the wall that led into the garden. It was quite warm; the ground steamed slightly, so that a faint mist hung low, and everything was wet, with but a dangerously narrow margin between the last splendour of autumn and its first sodden decay. She walked slowly up the garden path, looking at the bronze, red, yellow and orange flowers that were bent down towards the ground by the moisture; she walked up to the path, swinging her scissors, till she came to the clump of Scotch firs at the top of the garden, and stood surveying the country that swept down to the valley, rising to the Downs beyond, the woods in the valley golden through the mist, and blue smoke hanging above the deep violet pools of shadow, between the woods and the hills; all unstirred by any breath; rust-colour and blue in every shade from the pale tan of the stubble to the fire of the woods, from the wreathing smoke-blue to the depths of amethyst driven like wedges into the flanks of the Downs. Below the clump of Scotch firs the ground fell away rapidly; in the valley gleamed a sudden silver twist of the river. The river was Mrs. Martin's boundary, the natural frontier to her eight hundred acres. They had not always been eight hundred acres. Once they had only been five hundred, and only thanks to stringent frugality and a certain astuteness on Mrs. Martin's part had they been extended to that natural frontier which was the river. She could not think of that astuteness now without a measure of discomfort. Had she been *quite* as fair as she might have been—*quite* as scrupulous? Would she ever have persuaded Mr. Thistlethwaite to part with the required three hundred if she hadn't canvassed for him quite so enthusiastically before the poll? Was she quite sure that she agreed with all his political convictions? Was she even sure that she understood them? She dismissed these qualms, hurriedly and furtively, when they nudged her. Anyway, the three hundred acres were hers, and whatever she had done, she had done it for her son; let that be her defence in everything. She would bring him out here after luncheon, and he would stand looking over the valley, and possibly he would say, as he had said once before, years ago, "I wish our land went down as far as the river, don't you?" And then in a great moment she would reply "It does!" For she had never told him about the extra three hundred acres; she had kept that secret out of the long weekly letter she had written to him overseas during all the five years of his absence. There was no detail of her life that she hadn't told him; she had told him, separately, about each of her dinner parties; about the work on the farm, and about the agricultural experiments that she and Lynes, the bailiff, were making, their failure or their success; she had kept him informed of all the events in the village; but the three hundred

V. SACKVILLE-WEST

acres she had hugged to herself as a secret and a surprise. Lynes was her accomplice; she had had to warn him that he must never let out the secret should he have occasion to write to Mr. Henry. It had created a great link between herself and Lynes. There had, of course, been the danger that somebody or other in the district would be writing to Henry on other matters, and would mention his mother's purchase; but up to the present it was clear from Henry's letters that no one had done so. He had written to her with fair regularity, though not so often as she could have wished; but then she would have liked a letter by every mail, as he received from her, and that was unreasonable; and though sometimes his letters were brief, and clearly written in a hurry, she was too loyal to ask herself what he could possibly have to do with his evenings on a ranch where work would be finished by dusk.

She turned back along the path, and began cutting flowers wherewith she filled her basket. She cut very carefully where it would not show. No one else was allowed to cut the flowers. She was especially proud of this, her autumn border. On either side of the path, until it was brought up short at the end by the grey walls of the manor-house, it smouldered in broad bands that repeated the colours of the autumn woods. Orange snapdragon, marigold, and mimulus flowing forward on to the flagged path; then the bronze of coreopsis and helenium, stabbed by the lance-like spires of red-hot poker; and behind them the almost incredible brilliance of dahlias reared against the background of dark yew hedge. The border streamed away like a flaming tongue from the cool grey of the house. She had worked very hard and studied much to bring it to its present perfection; ten years of labour had at last been rewarded. Behind the yew hedges, to either side, were squares of old orchard, and the bright red apples nodded over the hedges like so many bright eyes peeping at the borders. In the grass under the apple-trees the bulbs lay dormant, that in the spring speckled the orchards with grape-hyacinths, anemones, and narcissi; but Mrs. Martin had forgotten about the spring. She was thinking, as she cut sheaves from the coreopsis and, more sparingly, from the snapdragons, that the autumn border was really the finest sight of the year, and that she was glad Henry should be coming now, and at no other time.

In the house, where she had everything conveniently arranged in the garden-room—a sink, taps, cloths for wiping the glasses, and a cupboard full of flower vases—she proceeded leisurely to do the flowers. No one had ever known Mrs. Martin be anything but leisurely; she always had plenty to occupy her time, but she was never hurried or ruffled. It was one of her greatest charms. She selected the flower vases with nice care; some were of rough pottery, but those now stood on one side, for she consecrated them to the spring flowers and to the roses; others were of glass, like green bubbles, glaucous and iridescent, light to the hand— for Mrs. Martin could not bear glasses that were not delicately blown, and as no one ever touched them except herself, they never got broken. She had a genius for handling fragility, quick and deft, and curiously tender. She was now wondering whether Henry's wife would some day stand in her place at the sink in the garden-room. She often wondered this, for Henry's wife was a personage she had long since absorbed into her thoughts. She thought of her without bitterness or jealousy, simply as a part of Henry, and consequently as another person to whom she would, in due course, have to hand over the house, the garden, and the estate—to render an account of her stewardship. Mrs. Martin was thinking about her as she snipped the ends off stalks that were too long, and lifted the vases that were already filled on to the tray standing ready to receive them. It made no difference that Henry should not yet have come across his wife; she was not thereby entitled, in Mrs. Martin's eyes, to any separate existence of her own. She was Henry's wife; the future mistress, when Mrs. Martin was dead, of the house and all it contained. It had taken a very long time for Mrs. Martin's mind to grow accustomed to this idea, but now that it was there she accepted it quite placidly, and it came up in its turn for examination amongst the other ideas, or was taken out when she wanted something to think about. She had even got into the way of saying to Lynes, or to the gardener, "I'm sure that Mrs. Henry would approve of that," and if, at first, they had been a little surprised, they had quickly come to take Mrs. Henry quite for granted. She had even an affection for Henry's wife. She liked to think of them living here together in the country, so far away from London—the country that was England although London forgot about it—and of Henry tramping over the eight hundred acres with a gun and a spaniel, while his wife stooped over the flowers in the walled garden, and she never doubted that they would frequently recall her, who had made the place what it was; recall her with a sort of grudging tenderness—she was too humanly wise a woman to expect more than that—and say, "The old lady ought to rest quietly in her grave. . ." She carried the tray of flowers into the hall, and from there distributed them; a big vase of coreopsis on each window sill in the sitting-room,

V. SACKVILLE-WEST

a bowl of marigolds on the table where the light of the lamp would fall straight on to them in the evening, a bowl of snapdragons in the centre of the hall, red and yellow nasturtiums on the dining-room table. There remained two little pots of snapdragon, which she took upstairs and put on the dressing-table in his bedroom. She came down again. The bronze of the flowers, she thought, suited the house, with its bits of oak panelling, the polished stairs of a golden-brown, and the pile carpet of mouse-brown in the sitting-room. She was pleased with her survey, though a little tired. She heaved the sigh of happy tiredness. Five years alone here, alone except for the neighbours; and although she liked being alone, and was quite content between Lynes and her garden in the daytime, and her books in the evening, she was very glad that Henry—who was really her unseen and constant companion, at the back of her mind in everything she did—should be coming back to her at last.

III

She watched the motor as it drove off to the station. She had had it opened, and had sent a number of coats and rugs with it lest Henry should be cold. By this time she was completely tired out, having pursued her self-imposed business down to its minutest detail, but the consciousness that she had done everything she had to do buoyed her up with the pleasure of virtue. Although she knew that she could not expect the motor back for at least half-an-hour, she enveloped herself in an old brown cape and went to sit on the little bench in the porch. The mist had by now been completely dispersed by the sun, which had rolled it away in curls and shavings of vapour, that clung about the trees as though reluctant to go, and finally melted away, leaving a day full of damp gold, with the pheasants calling in the distance along the margins of the fields nearest to the coppices. Mrs. Martin sat in the porch with her feet propped up on the opposite bench. She rested contentedly, folding her old brown cloak round her, and letting her head nod under its big black straw hat as she dozed. She looked like some old shepherd nodding after his dinner hour. The pigeons came and pecked about under her feet for stray grains of maize, and were joined by some chickens from the farmyard that came scurrying across the court, the big Rhode Island Reds and the white Wyandottes with their bright yellow legs prinking round and squawking as all their heads met in a rush over the same grain. Mrs. Martin smiled as she dozed, like a mother smiling indulgently at the squabble of her children. The sunlight fell in a sharp line across the flag-stone of the porch. Little bright drops of moisture formed on the hairy tweed of Mrs. Martin's cloak where her gentle and regular breathing blew down the front of it. She had not meant to go to sleep. She would not have believed that she could go to sleep while she was actually waiting for the arrival of Henry. Five years—and then, at the end of it, to sleep! But she was old, and she had been busy all the morning, and she was tired. She slept on, with the pigeons and chickens still pecking, quietly now, under her feet.

IV

Henry was there; he arrived cheerful and full of good-will. If, coming down in the train—three hours; how could anyone, good Lord, so bury themselves in the country when they weren't obliged to?— if, coming down in the train, he had drilled himself rather deliberately into the suitable frame of mind, at the actual moment of his arrival he found himself unexpectedly invaded by a rush of genuine pleasure. He had been touched by the sudden sight of his mother asleep in the porch, wrapped in the same old cloak which he well remembered; her cheek, when he kissed it, had been so cool and soft and naturally scented; and her confusion and delight had both been so sweet and so candid. They went into the house together, eagerly; he put down his hat and coat on the same coffer which was in its unaltered place, and still the warmth of homecoming had not deserted him. She took his arm and led him towards the sitting-room, "Not much change, you see, Henry; I had to have new covers for the chairs and the sofa, and I thought it would be nice to have them a little different, but everything else is just the same. Now I expect you'd like to go to your room and wash: I've had some hot water put there for you; and luncheon will be ready in five minutes."

He splashed over his basin, looking round his room meanwhile and thinking how clean and fresh it was, and how jolly the view out of the window with the river shining down in the valley, washing his hands with an energy that brought the soap up into an instant lather, and as he dried them on the soft huckaback of the fringed towel he smiled to himself, for he remembered the old joke of his mother's niceness over such things as linen. He unpacked his brushes and brushed his hair vigorously; it was sleek and black, and he brushed it till it shone like a top-hat. He ran downstairs, jumping the last six steps and shouting out to his mother. He felt quite boyish. He put his hand through her arm and drew her out to the porch, where they stood while they waited for luncheon. He held her arm close to his side in a possessive way. They were both very gay, and rather tremulous.

V

How well you look, Henry! and so brown; why, you might be twenty instead of nearly thirty. Now what do you want to drink? claret, beer, cider. . . Try a little of our cider, it's home-made, last season's brew, and I think we have got in exactly the right measure of wheat. It is so easy to make a mistake—to put in too little or too much—but I think last autumn we got it just right."

But Henry did not care for cider; he preferred whisky and soda.

"Have what you like, of course, dear boy. Here are my keys, Sandford; get the bottle of whisky out of my cupboard, please, and bring it for Mr. Henry, and let me have the keys back. Dear me, Henry, we both have so much to say to one another that it makes us quite silent. I scarcely know where to begin. Never mind, it will all come out little by little, and we have plenty of time before us. I have made a great plan of all I want to show you this afternoon; you must come round to the farm after luncheon and speak to Lynes, and I daresay he will like to have a whole day with you, going over things, tomorrow or the day after that. . ."

She beamed at him where he sat opposite to her, at the end of the table, and he smiled back at her; she thought how nice-looking he was, with his lean, brown face and black hair. He had the look of hard health; she remembered how well he had always looked in the saddle. It had, indeed, been a great incentive to have this son to work for; to guard his interests, to build up the perfect little estate for him to inherit. The studious evenings she had spent had not been wasted; all that she had learnt, conscientiously—for she would never trust wholly to Lynes' experience—about manures, the rotation of crops, the value of luzerne, the advantage of fat stock over dairy-produce, all that laboriously acquired knowledge, in the service of such a son, had not been useless. It wasn't in the nature of women, she had decided long ago, to work solely for the sake of the work; and this was one of the things she often said, particularly when the subject of women's emancipation was mentioned. How impressed he would be, after luncheon, when she took him out! He would expect her to know about the garden; the garden had always been her speciality; but he should find that she wasn't a docile ignoramus about the farm, a mere writer of cheques to Lynes' dictation. She beamed at him again, hugging her satisfaction to herself. She was glad that she had not been born a man, to work for work's own cold, ungrateful sake, but a woman, to work for the warm appreciation in a fellow-being's eyes.

And Henry was charming her, as she had expected to be charmed. He chaffed her a little, and she fell into a little confusion, not knowing whether to take him seriously, until she perceived that he was laughing and then she reproached him for teasing an old woman and they laughed happily together. He saw that he was being a success, and expanded under the flattery. He teased her about her old cloak; she found an exquisite thrill in the proprietary intimacy with which this man, who was like a stranger to her, was treating her. She blushed and bridled; and the more she bridled the more fondly he teased. His eyes were narrowed into laughing slits; he leant over to her as he might have leant, confidentially, over to any woman with whom he happened to be lunching. She thought, with a queer envy, of the future Mrs. Henry; and the thought made her ask, abruptly, "You've nothing to tell me about yourself? You're not engaged, I mean, or thinking of it?"

Henry looked taken aback by the question; then he threw back his head and laughed.

"Good Lord, who to? You forget I've been in the heart of the Argentine for five years."

"Oh no, I don't forget," she said softly, thinking how little she had forgotten, "but one finds old friends in London. . . I don't know. . ."

For a moment he seemed embarrassed; it passed.

"I've not been in London forty-eight hours and I had plenty of other things to do there." He said it glibly, hoping she would not wonder what he had done with his evenings. She did not wonder, her imagination not readily extending to restaurants or dancing places, or the bare shoulders of women under a slipping opera cloak. She had forgotten about those things; it was so long since they had come her way, even remotely. And in spite of her benevolence towards Mrs. Henry she was conscious of a fugitive relief.

"Then I needn't feel selfish about keeping you here," she said, "and it will be a nice rest for you after your journey and all the business you had to do in London. Now if you have quite finished, we might go out? It gets dark so quickly." They went out; already the fresh beauty of the day was passing, it was colder, and there was more grey and less gold between the trees. "Let us go up to the top of the garden," said Mrs. Martin, who felt she could not bear to keep the secret of the three hundred acres to herself a moment longer.

VI

They went slowly up the garden path between the flaming borders, that flamed less now that the sun was no longer on them. She noted the difference, and was sorry they should not be showing themselves off at their best. Nevertheless Henry said, "How jolly your flowers are, mother," and she was satisfied. She had taken his arm; from her other hand swung her inseparable companion, the garden basket, and from sheer habit she kept a sharp look out for a possible weed. Even though Henry was there. She knew now—now that he was there—how lonely had been her wanderings up that garden path, and how hollow, really, had been her gardening triumphs since there was no one to admire them and to share. Not that she had ever faced the fact; for it was not her habit to face facts. But now, since it had become a fact only in the past, she could allow herself to turn round and wave it a little belated, valedictory gesture of recognition. She pressed Henry's arm ever so slightly against her side. Not enough for him to notice; only enough to give herself assurance and comfort. Stupid of her not to have realized how much she wanted Henry. He had been always in the background, of course, and she had trained herself to think that that was enough; perhaps it was fortunate, rather than stupid; she would have wanted him too much, if once she had let herself begin to think about it. It was pleasant to have the physical support of his arm to lean on; it was surprisingly pleasant to have the moral support of his presence. She had had to carry all the responsibility herself for so long, the responsibility of decisions, all the loneliness of command; and although she was quite well aware of her own efficiency she felt that she was growing a little tired, and would be happy to let some of the responsibility slide off on to Henry's shoulders. When Lynes was obstinate, as he sometimes was, it would be a comfort to reply that he must discuss the matter with Mr. Henry. At the end of this train of thought she said confidently to Henry, "You won't be going back to the Argentine anymore, dear, will you?"

Henry emerged startled from a parallel train of thought that he had been following. The first warm excitement of his homecoming had passed, and he was beginning to wonder what he should do, when once his mother had had her fill of showing him all which she had vaguely threatened to show, and which he did not particularly want to see. Already, with reaction, things were a little flat. But he answered, without any perceptible pause, "No, no more Argentine for me. I'm fed up with the place." He was; the solitude, the rough life, had not been to his taste; he had grown to hate the plains, and the stupid, ubiquitous cattle, and the endless cattle-talk. No more Argentine for him; he had had the experience, he had made the money he wanted to make, now he wanted the pleasure to which he thought he was entitled.

"That's nice," said Mrs. Martin comfortably; "it will be nice for me to have you at home in my old age."

Henry let this remark pass; he hated inflicting disappointment, and there would be plenty of time in which to make his plans clear to his mother. In the meantime she was so obviously happy; a pity to throw a shadow over her first day.

They reached the top of the path and the clump of firs. Mrs. Martin's heart was beating hard, and a little pink flush had appeared on her cheeks. It was not, after all, everyday that one reached a moment one had anticipated for nearly five years. She wished she had had the strength of mind to wait until the following morning before bringing Henry here, for the country was lovelier under the morning mists than now in the cruder light of the afternoon; but she had been too much excited, too impatient. They stood there looking down over the valley, across it to the Downs. She let him look his fill.

"Better than the Argentine, Henry?"

"By Jove, yes, I should think so: better than the Argentine."

She gave a chuckle of happiness. She dealt her secret out to him in small doses, like the old Epicurean she was.

"Isn't it nice to think, Henry, that those fields and woods belong to you?"

"But they don't," he said, "they belong to you."

"Well—doesn't that amount to the same thing?"

"Oh, no," he said, "not at all the same thing," and the difference in his mind was that whereas she loved and wanted the fields and woods, their possession would have bored him.

"Dear Henry, that is just an evasion. You know that it amounts to the same thing really. Let us, for the sake of argument, assume that they belong to us both."

"All right," he said, humouring her.

"Do you remember," she went on, "we used to say, how nice it would be if our property went down as far as the river?"

"Did we?—Doesn't it?—No, I don't remember," he said absently.

"But, Henry! Think, darling! Well, it does now: right down to the river."

"How splendid!" he replied, feeling that he was expected to say something of the sort. "But didn't it always?"

VII

S he went into no explanation; she did not remind him of the three hundred acres required to round off the estate, nor did she make the confession which she had been saving up, like a guilty child, of how she had got round the obstinacy of Mr. Thistlethwaite. She made some quiet reply to his last remark, and went on talking of other things. He was perfectly oblivious to the moment that had come and gone. And she, in her mind, was already making excuses for him; he had been away for so long, he had grown accustomed to such vast districts where three hundred acres must seem paltry indeed! When they had looked sufficiently at the view, she returned down the path beside him, her hand still slipped into the crook of his arm, without the slightest resentment. Henry! she could never harbour resentment against Henry.

But a little of the eagerness was gone; not much; only the first edge taken off. She struggled to restore it; she had an uneasy feeling of disloyalty towards Henry. And really he had been so very charming; nothing could have been more charming or more to her taste than his manner towards her from the very first moment when he had bent to kiss her in the porch, fond but deferential, intimate but courteous. Henry was the sort of man who would always be courteous towards women, even when the woman happened to be his own mother. Mrs. Martin greatly appreciated courtesy. She often said that it was becoming rarer and more rare. Certainly, Henry's manner had been perfect in every respect, and she was seized with remorse that she could have directed against him so much as the criticism of a passing disappointment. She must not admit to herself that the edge of her eagerness was blunted; and she began forcing herself to talk of Lynes and the farm, and presently, because Henry listened with so much attention and interest, she found her eagerness creeping back. They went round to the rickyard together, where Lynes, in his breeches and leather gaiters, was talking to the carter, but broke off to come towards Henry, who shook hands with him while Mrs. Martin stood by, beaming upon their meeting. She was enchanted with Henry; he asked Lynes questions about the cattle, and followed him into the door of the shed where the afternoon's milking was in progress. Mrs. Martin waited for them near the ricks, because she did not like the dirty cobbles of the farmyard; she was perfectly happy again; this was what she had always foreseen, and she liked things to turn out exactly according to the picture she had been in the habit of making in advance in her own mind; she was only disconcerted when they fell out differently. How good was Henry's manner with Lynes! she watched the two men as they stood in the doorway of the cowshed; Henry had said something and Lynes was laughing; he pushed back his cap off his forehead and scratched his head, and she heard him say, "That's right, sir, that's just about the size of it." Her heart swelled with pride in Henry. He was getting on with Lynes; Lynes approved of him, that was obvious, and Lynes' approval was not easily won. He was a scornful man, not always very tractable either, and very contemptuous of most people's knowledge of agriculture; but here he was approving of Henry. Her own esteem of Henry rose in proportion as she saw Lynes' esteem. She felt that a little of the credit belonged to her for being Henry's mother.

They came towards her, walking slowly and talking, across the soft ground of the rickyard, where the cartwheels had cut deep ruts and the wisps of straw were sodden into the black earth. It was a great satisfaction to her to see Henry and Lynes thus together. She was the impresario exhibiting them to one another. The afternoon was drawing very gently to a close. A little cold, perhaps, a little grey, but still tender; a dove-like grey, hovering over the trees, over the ricks, and over the barn with the yellow lichen on the roof. A tang of damp farmyard was, not unpleasantly, on the air.

"We'll go in now, shall we, Henry? It's getting chilly," said Mrs. Martin, wrapping herself more closely in her brown cloak, and nodding and smiling to Lynes.

As they went towards the house, Henry said, looking down at her in that confidential way he had, "Well, that's a great duty accomplished, isn't it?"

"Duty, Henry?"

"Yes. Talking to Lynes, I mean."

"Oh! talking to Lynes. To be sure—You were so nice to him, dear boy; thank you."

Duty—the word gave her a small chill. She bent over the fire in the sitting-room, poking it into a blaze; the logs fell apart and shot up into flame.

"I do like a wood fire," said Mrs. Martin. She held out her hands towards it; they were cold. She had not known, until that moment, how cold she had been.

VIII

They were at dinner. How nice Henry looked in his evening clothes; she liked his lean brown hands, and the gesture with which he smoothed back his hair. She smiled fondly as she thought how attractive all women must find Henry. Life on a ranch had not coarsened him; far from it. He was sensitive and masculine both, an ideal combination.

"Dear Henry!" she murmured.

He leant over and patted her hand, but there was an absent look in his eyes, and his manner was slightly more perfunctory than it had been at luncheon. Anyone but Mrs. Martin would have suspected that he could assume that manner at will—had, in fact, assumed it often, towards many women who had misinterpreted it, and whom he had forgotten as soon as they were out of sight. They had reproached him sometimes; there was a fair echo of reproaches in Henry's life. He had always felt aggrieved when they reproached him; couldn't they understand that he was kind-hearted really? that he only wanted to please? To make life agreeable? He hated saying anything disagreeable to anybody, but greatly preferred enrolling them among the victims of his charm—which he could turn on, at a moment's notice, like turning on a tap—and if they misunderstood him, he did not consider that he had been to blame. Not that he remained to argue the matter out. It was far easier, in most cases, simply to go right away instead, without giving any explanation, right away to where the clamour that was sure to arise would not reach his ears at all. And sometimes, when he had not managed so skilfully as usual, and things had been, briefly, tiresome, he would criticize himself to the extent of thinking that he was a damned fool to have, incorrigibly, so little foresight of where the easy path was leading him.

Yet he was not quite right about this, for he was perfectly well able to recognize the progress of his own drifting; but he recognized it as though it applied to someother person, in whose affairs he was himself unable to interfere. He watched himself as he might have watched another man, thinking meanwhile, with an amused contempt and a certain compassion, "How the dickens is he going to get himself out of this?"

IX

He could, if he had been so inclined, have observed the process at work after dinner, when, his mother seated with knitting in an arm-chair on the one side of the fire, and he with a cigar in another arm-chair on the other side of the fire, his legs stretched out straight to the blaze, they talked intermittently, a conversation in which the future played more part than the past. Henry found that his mother had definite ideas about the future, ideas which she took for granted that he would share. He knew that he ought to say at once that he did not share them; but that would entail disappointing his mother, and this he was reluctant to do—at any rate on the first day. Poor old lady—let her be happy. What was the good of sending her to bed worried? In a day or two he would give her a hint. He remembered that she was not usually slow at taking a hint. He hoped she would not make a fuss. Really, it would be unreasonable if she made a fuss; she could not seriously expect him to spend his life in talking to Lynes! But for the present, let her keep her illusions; she seemed so greatly to enjoy telling him about her farm, and he needn't listen; he could say "Yes," and "Fancy," from time to time, since that seemed to satisfy her, and, meanwhile, he could think about Isabel. He had promised Isabel that he would not be away for more than three days at the outside. He hoped he would not find it too difficult to get away back to London at the end of three days; there would be a fuss if he went, but on the other hand Isabel would make a far worse fuss if he stayed. Isabel was not as easy-going as he could have wished, though her flares of temper, when they were not so prolonged as to become inconvenient, amused him and constituted part of the attraction she had for him. He rendered to Isabel the homage that she attracted him just as much now as five years ago, before he left for the Argentine. She had even improved in the interval; improved with experience, he told himself cynically, not resenting the experience in the least; she had improved in appearance too, having found her type; and he recalled the shock of delight with which he had seen her again: the curious pale eyes, and the hard line of the clubbed black hair, cut square across her brows; certainly Isabel had attraction, and was as wild as she could be, not a woman one could neglect with impunity, if one didn't want her to be off and away. . . No. There was a flick and a spirit about Isabel; that was what he liked. How his mother would

V. SACKVILLE-WEST

disapprove of Isabel! he sent out, to disguise a little chuckle, a long stream of smoke, and the thought of his mother's disapproval tickled him much. His mother, rambling on about foot-and-mouth disease, and about how afraid they had been, last year, that it would come across into Gloucestershire, while Isabel, probably, was at some supper-party sitting on a table and singing to her guitar those Moorish songs in her husky, seductive voice. He was not irritated with his mother for her difference; at another moment he might have been irritated; but at present he was too comfortable, too warm, too full of a good dinner, to find her unconsciousness anything but diverting; and, as the contrast appeared to him more and more as a good joke, he encouraged her with sympathetic comments and with the compliment of his grave attention, so that she put behind her finally and entirely the disappointment she had had over the three hundred acres, and expounded to him all her dearest schemes, leaning forward tapping him on the knee with her long knitting-needle to enforce her points, enlisting his sympathy in all her difficulties with Lynes and Lynes' obstinacy, exactly as she had planned to do, and as, up to the present, she had not secured a very good opportunity of doing. This was ideal: to sit by the fireside after dinner with Henry, long, slender, nodding gravely, his eyes on the fire intent with concentration, and to pour out to him all the little grievances of years, and the satisfactions too, for she did not believe in dwelling only upon what went wrong, but also upon that which went right.

"And so you see, dear boy, I have really been able to make both ends meet; it was a little difficult at times, I own, but now I am bound to say the farm is paying very nicely. Lynes could show you the account-books, anytime; I think perhaps you ought to run your eye over them. You must have picked up a lot of useful knowledge, out there?"

"Oh yes," said Henry, broadly.

"Well, it will all come in very useful here, won't it? although I daresay English practice is different in many ways. I could see that Lynes very quickly discovered that you knew what you were talking about. It will be a great thing for me, Henry, a very great thing, to have your support and advice in future."

Henry made an attempt; he said, "But if I don't happen to be on the spot?"

"Oh, well, you won't be very far away," said Mrs. Martin comfortably. "Even if you do like to have rooms in London I could always get you at a moment's notice."

Henry found great consolation in this remark; it offered a loophole, and he readily placed his faith in loopholes. He was also relieved, because he considered, his mother having said that, there was no necessity now for him to say anything. Let her prattle about the estate, and about the use he was going to be to her; there would always be, now, those rooms in London in which he could take refuge. "Why, you suggested it yourself," he could say, raising aggrieved eyebrows, if any discussion arose in the future. It was true that her next observations diminished the value of his loophole, but he chose to ignore that; what was said, was said. Rooms in London, Christmas with his mother, and perhaps a week-end in the summer, and a couple of days' shooting in the autumn; he wouldn't mind a little rough shooting, and had already ascertained from Lynes that there were a good many partridges and a few pheasants; and he could always take back some birds to Isabel. He saw himself, on the station platform, with his flat gun-case and cartridge bag, and the heavy bundle of limp game, rabbits, partridges, and pheasants tied together by the legs. He would go out tomorrow, and see what he could pick up for Isabel. His mother would never object; she would think the game was for his own use, in those rooms she, thank goodness, so conveniently visualized. And if it wasn't for Isabel, in future years, well, no doubt it would be for somebody else.

He awoke from these plans to what his mother was saying.

"I don't think it would be good for you to live entirely in the country. So I shall drive you away, Henry dear, whenever you show signs of becoming a vegetable. I shall be able to carry on perfectly well without you, as I have done all these years. You need never worry about that. Besides, you must go to London to look for Mrs. Henry."

"What?" said Henry, genuinely startled.

His mother, said, smiling, that some day he would have to marry. She would like to know her grandchildren before she died. There was the long attic at the top of the house which they could have as a playroom.

"Sure there is no one?" she questioned him again, more urgently, more archly this time, and he denied it laughing, to reassure her; and suddenly the laughter which he had affected, became hearty, for he had thought of Isabel, Isabel whom he would never dream of marrying, and who would never dream of marrying him; Isabel, insolent, lackadaisical, exasperating, with the end of a cigarette—a fag, she called it—smouldering between her lips; Isabel with her hands stuck in the pockets of her velveteen jacket, and her short black hair; Isabel holding forth, perched on the corner of a table, contradicting him, getting angry, pushing him away when he tried to catch hold of her and kiss her—"Oh, you think the idea of marrying funny enough now," said his mother sagely, hearing him laugh, "but you may be coming to me with a very different tale in a few months' time."

He was in a thoroughly good temper by now; he lounged deeper into his arm-chair and stirred the logs with his foot. "Good cigars these, mother," he said, critically examining the one he took from between his teeth; "who advises you about cigars?"

"Mr. Thistlethwaite recommended those," Mrs. Martin replied enchanted.

"Mr. Thistlethwaite? Who's Mr. Thistlethwaite?" asked Henry.

She had an impulse to tell him, even now, the story of Mr. Thistlethwaite and the three hundred acres; to ask him whether he thought she had acted very unscrupulously; but a funny inexplicable pride held her back. She said quietly that Mr. Thistlethwaite was the local M.P. Henry, to her relief, betrayed no further interest. He continued to stir the fire absently with the toe of his shoe, and his mother, watching him, looked down a long vista of such evenings, when the lamplight would fall on to the bowl of flowers she placed so skilfully to receive it, and on the black satin head of Henry.

X

She opened her window before getting into bed, and looked out upon a clear night and the low-lying mists of autumn. It was very still; the church clock chimed, a dog barked in the distance, and the breathless silence spread once more like a lake round the ripple of those sounds. She looked towards that bit of England which was sufficient to her, milky and invisible; she thought of the ricks standing in the silent rickyard, and the sleeping beasts near by in the sheds; she, who had been brisk and practical for so many years, became a little dreamy. Then bestirring herself, she crossed the room to bed. All was in order: a glass of milk by the bed, a box of matches, a clean handkerchief, her big repeater watch. She wound it carefully, and put it away under the many pillows. She sank luxuriously into the pillows—that little pleasure which was every night renewed. She thought to herself that she was really almost too happy; such happiness was a pain; there was no means of expressing it; she could not shout and sing, so it had to be bottled up, and the compression was pain, exquisitely. For about five minutes, during which she lived, with a swimming head, through a lifetime of sensations, she lay awake; then amongst her pillows she fell asleep.

XI

Next morning she was awakened by some sound she could not at first define, but which she presently identified as the remote ringing of the telephone bell. She listened. The servants would answer it, of course, but she wondered who could be calling the house so early in the day. Feeling very wide awake she slipped into her dressing-gown and slippers and went to the top of the stairs to listen. She heard Henry's voice, downstairs in the hall.

"Yes, yes, hullo. Yes, I'm here. Is that you, darling? Sorry to ring you up at this hour, but later on every word I said would be overheard. Yes, infernally public." He laughed softly. "No, I don't suppose anyone ever uses this telephone for purposes they'd rather keep to themselves. Oh, all right, thanks. Pleased to see me? Yes, I think so. Look here, things are going to be deuced awkward. Well, she expects me to spend most of my time here—Yes, an awful bore—Oh, well, it's natural enough, I suppose. Five years, and all that, don't you know. Well, but what am I to say? Can't be too brutal, can one?—Oh, bored stiff in two days, of course, I simply don't know what to do about it. Besides, I'm dying to get back to you.—Yes, silly, of course.—I wish you'd help, Isabel. Tell me what to say to the old lady.—No, she seems to take it quite for granted. Oh, all the year round, with an occasional week in London.—I can't say I think it in the least funny.—Well, of course, if I was a downright brute. . ."

Mrs. Martin turned and went back into her bedroom. She shut the door very gently behind her. Presently she heard Henry come upstairs and go into his room.

THE PARROT

To H. G. N.

I

O nce upon a time there was a small green parrot, with a coral-coloured head. It should have lived in Uruguay, but actually it lived in Pimlico, in a cage, a piece of apple stuck between the bars at one end of its perch, and a lump of sugar between the bars at the other. It was well-cared for; its drinking water was fresh everyday, the seed in its little trough was daily renewed, and the cage stood on a table in the window to get the yellow sunlight that occasionally penetrated the muslin curtains. The room, furthermore, was well-warmed, and all cats and such dangers kept rigorously away. In spite of all this, the bird was extremely disagreeable. If anyone went to stand beside its cage, in order to admire its beautiful and brilliant colouring, it took refuge in a corner, buried its head beneath the seed-trough, and screamed on a harsh, shrill note like a pig in the shambles. Whenever it believed itself to be unobserved, it returned to the eternal and unavailing occupation of trying to get out of its cage.

In early days, it had had a cage of less substantial make: being a strong little bird it had contrived to loosen a bar and to make its escape once or twice into the room; but, consequent on this, a more adequate cage had been procured, the bars of which merely twanged like harp-strings under the assault of the beak, and yielded not at all. Nevertheless the parrot was not discouraged. It had twenty-four hours out of everyday at its disposal, and three hundred and sixty-five days out of every year. It worked at the bars with its beak; it stuck its feet against the sides, and tugged at the bar. Once it discovered how to open the door, after which the door had to be secured with a piece of string. The owners of the parrot explained to it, that, should it make good its escape from the house, it would surely fall a prey to a cat, a dog, or a passing motor; and if to none of these things, then to the climate of England, which in no way resembled the climate of Uruguay. When they stood beside its cage giving those explanations, it got down into the corner, cowered, and screamed.

The parrot was looked after by the under-housemaid, a slatternly girl of eighteen, with smudges of coal on her apron, and a smear of violet eyes in a white sickly face. She used to talk to the parrot while she was cleaning out the tray at the bottom of the cage, confiding to it all her perplexities, which she could safely do without fear of being overheard, by reason of the din the parrot maintained meanwhile. In spite of its lack of response, she had for the parrot a passion which transformed it into a symbol. Its jade-green and coral seemed to give her a hint of something marvellously far removed from Pimlico. Her fifteen minutes with the parrot every morning remained the one fabulous excursion of her day; it was a journey to Bagdad, a peep into the caves of Aladdin. "Casting down their golden crowns upon a glassy sea," she murmured, in a hotch-potch of religion and romance—for the two in her mind were plaited together into an unexplained but beautiful braid, that was a source of confusion, rapture, and a strange unhappiness.

Apart from the function of cleaning out the cage, which she performed with efficiency, she was, considered as a housemaid, a failure. Perpetually in trouble, she tried to mend her ways; would turn energetic, would scrub and polish; then, as she relapsed into daydreams, the most important part of her work would be left forgotten. Scolding and exasperation stormed around her ears. Sometimes she appeared disheartened and indifferent; sometimes she gazed in a scared fashion at the indignant authority and set about her work with a dazed vehemence. But black-lead and Brasso remained to her, in spite of her efforts, of small significance.

Meanwhile the parrot gave up the attempt to get out of its cage, and spent its days moping upon the topmost perch.

II

Peace reigned in the house. The parrot no longer tore at its bars or screamed, and as for the under-housemaid, she was a transformed creature: punctual, orderly, competent, and unobtrusive. The cook said she didn't know what had come over the bird and the girl. According to her ideas, the situation was now most satisfactory. The two rebels had at last fallen into line with the quiet conduct of the house, and there was no longer anything to complain of, either in the sitting-room or the basement. It would have been hypercritical to complain that the girl's quietness was disconcerting. When her tasks were done, she retired to her bedroom, where she might be found at any moment sitting with her hands lying in her lap, the violet eyes looking out of the window. Well, if she chose so to spend her time. . . The parrot sat huddled on its perch, flaunting in plumage indeed, for that was beyond its control, but irreproachable in demeanour. It appeared almost to apologize by its humility for the garishness of colour wherewith Nature had afflicted it.

One morning the cook came down as was her custom, and found the following note addressed to her, propped up on the kitchen dresser:

> Dear Mrs. White,
>   i have gone to wear the golden crown but i have lit the stokhole and laid the brekfast.

Very much annoyed, and wondering what tricks the girl had been up to, she climbed the stairs to the girl's bedroom. The room had been tidied, and the slops emptied away, and the girl was lying dead upon the bed.

She flew downstairs with the news. In the sitting-room, where she collided with her mistress, she noticed the parrot on its back on the floor of the cage, its two little legs sticking stiffly up into the air.

A Note About the Author

V. Sackville-West (1892–1952) was an English novelist, poet, journalist, and gardener. Born at Knole, the Sackville's hereditary home in west Kent, Vita was the daughter of English peer Lionel Sackville-West and his cousin Victoria, herself the illegitimate daughter of the 2nd Baron Sackville and a Spanish dancer named Pepita. Educated by governesses as a young girl, Vita later attended school in Mayfair, where she met her future lover Violet Keppel. An only child, she entertained herself by writing novels, plays, and poems in her youth, both in English and French. At the age of eighteen, she made her debut in English society and was courted by powerful and well-connected men. She had affairs with men and women throughout her life, leading an open marriage with diplomat Harold Nicholson. Following their wedding in 1913, the couple moved to Constantinople for one year before returning to settle in England, where they raised two sons. Vita's most productive period of literary output, in which she published such works as *The Land* (1926) and *All Passion Spent* (1931), coincided with her affair with English novelist Virginia Woolf, which lasted from 1925 to 1935. The success of Vita's writing—published through Woolf's Hogarth Press—allowed her lover to publish some of her masterpieces, including *The Waves* (1931) and *Orlando* (1928), the latter being inspired by Sackville-West's family history, androgynous features, and unique personality. Vita died at the age of seventy at Sissinghurst Castle, where she worked with her husband to design one of England's most famous gardens.

A Note from the Publisher

Spanning many genres, from non-fiction essays to literature classics to children's books and lyric poetry, Mint Edition books showcase the master works of our time in a modern new package. The text is freshly typeset, is clean and easy to read, and features a new note about the author in each volume. Many books also include exclusive new introductory material. Every book boasts a striking new cover, which makes it as appropriate for collecting as it is for gift giving. Mint Edition books are only printed when a reader orders them, so natural resources are not wasted. We're proud that our books are never manufactured in excess and exist only in the exact quantity they need to be read and enjoyed.

bookfinity™

Discover more of your favorite classics with Bookfinity™.

- Track your reading with custom book lists.
- Get great book recommendations for your personalized Reader Type.
- Add reviews for your favorite books.
- AND MUCH MORE!

Visit **bookfinity.com** and take the fun Reader Type quiz to get started.

Enjoy our classic and modern companion pairings!